DEAD IN VENICE

FIONA LEITCH

PROLOGUE

I flipped open the laptop, offered up a silent prayer to the God of CrimeWriters, Our Lord Jesus Agatha Christ(ie), and started my new novel. Again...

DCI FLETCHER MURDER MYSTERY 6 by Annabelle Tyson (Working title – *Only Writing This One For The Money*)

It was a warm night. A gentle breeze rippled the surface of the murky waters of the Thames, shattering reflections of the lights on Tower Bridge into a crazy myriad of – of – of something. I'll come back to that. You don't need to know about the breeze though, do you? This is a crime novel, not the sodding five-day weather forecast. Anyway –

Oh yes. Warm night. River Thames near Tower Bridge.

DCI Daisy Fletcher leant over the railings and watched the reflections dance, her long auburn hair curling over her shoulders in a tumbling, frothing cascade of – oh bollocks. Not actual bollocks, obviously. That would be weird and anatomically unlikely.

She looked at her watch. It was time. He was never late. And tonight was no exception.

She felt, rather than heard him approach – he trod softly for a tall man – and turned imperceptibly towards him.

"Ze black svan sings Abba at karaoke," he said. His accent – St Petersburg via Berlin via every other goddamn spy thriller location – was still exotic enough to her to send a thrill coursing down her spine, despite the ridiculous words. She cursed herself for not being immune to dark hair, a swarthy complexion and a stature of 6'2". She didn't answer, wanting – needing – to hear him speak again.

A slight quiver of irritation betrayed him.

"Ze black svan sings Abba at karaoke," he insisted, and this time the ludicrous words penetrated her brain.

"I'm not doing it," she said.

He sighed. "You has to," he said, sounding aggrieved. They'd had this conversation before. "It is ze password."

"All right, all right, don't get your balalaika in a twist!" She looked across the river, gritted her teeth and spoke the words.

"Gimme gimme gimme a man after midnight. There, satisfied? We both look stupid now. Who comes up with these passwords anyway? Is there a whole department at Interpol dedicated to making their agents look like arsewits? Or do they just not like you?"

"DCI Fletcher, ifs you are going to take my piss – "

"No, no, no, I'm sorry Viktor. Now what is so important that you risk your cover to come and find me?"

Viktor looked around, nervously. "I have to tell you – "

"Yes?"

"I have to tell you – "

"What?"

Viktor's voice suddenly changed to that of a middle aged, single, slightly overweight female novelist who hadn't had sex in a long time and was addicted to Chocolate Hobnobs.

"I have to tell you that this is the biggest load of shite you've ever written, and that's saying something."

CHAPTER ONE

I looked at the laptop in disgust and collapsed in a heap of self-loathing, banging my head on the desk. It hurt, but I probably deserved it for unleashing that derivative bollocks on the world.

I lay there for a moment, unable to do anything more than moan in despair, then sat bolt upright and faced the laptop again. I highlighted the words on the screen.

"Right! You're being deleted. And you. Die, you pile of crap! And you. And – oh sod it." I closed the file – DCI Fletcher Murder Mystery No 6 - then dragged the whole thing to the Trash, emptying it before I could change my mind. "That'll learn you," I said, my voice sounding very loud in the empty room. In the empty house.

I stared at the screen for a moment feeling vaguely dissatisfied, before glancing thoughtfully over at the old typewriter salvaged out of my Nana's attic when I was a penniless aspiring writer, on the other side of the study. I wrote my first novel on that typewriter with its sticky 'P'. It was old tech, but writing on it had always felt satisfyingly clunky; it required some physical as well as mental effort on the part of the writer and made you feel like Hemingway. And of course, when you ballsed it up, was there anything more liberating then ripping out the sheet of paper and tearing it up into tiny bits? And then throwing the tiny bits up into the air like literary confetti, and then dancing on the tiny bits, and then crawling around under the desk trying to pick up the tiny bits, and then giving up and getting the Hoover out to vacuum up the tiny bits –

I am going mental I thought to myself, not wanting to speak out loud again and remind myself how quiet the house was. This was followed by *I wonder if there are any chocolate biscuits left* but I was kidding myself. I knew there wasn't even a digestive to be had. With a sigh of resignation, I shut the laptop and went down the shops.

Writer's block is the pits. A writer with writer's block is like Casanova with erectile dysfunction. You get yourself all worked up, thinking about what you're going to do, fantasising about your fingers getting to work; you take yourself off upstairs, assume the position, and then – nothing.

Nothing happens.

Or worse, a pathetic spume of flaccid prose leaks out onto the page and stares back at you, accusingly, as if to say *"is THAT it?"*

Of course, a first draft is SUPPOSED to suck. It's supposed to consist of great swathes of turgid crap, strung together by the occasional pearl of sheer brilliance and breath-taking wit. And then you refine and tweak and rework until it's a bright shiny nugget of awesomeness you can see your face in. There's a saying in literary circles: writing is mostly rewriting.

Unfortunately there's another saying that goes, "You can't polish a turd."

There was a package waiting for me when I got back from the corner shop. I wasn't expecting anything, but I have been known to go into a trance and randomly buy stuff off eBay when bored, so I didn't think anything of it. I picked it up and went indoors.

I toyed with the idea of going straight back up to my study and getting back to work, but soon dismissed that as possibly the worst idea I'd had today, although the day was still young and there was plenty of time for me to come up with a worse one. I needed new stories, new characters – DCI Fletcher had won me awards and made me enough money to buy this rather nice house, even after the divorce settlement, but she was starting to get stale. She'd faced serial killers, terrorists, Russian spies, Jihadists, sneaky government officials, a bastard ex-husband (write what you know, my old English teacher used to say) and – yawn – her own inner demons, but so far she was proving no match for my creative constipation.

What I really needed at the moment, I decided, was a cup of tea and some rubbish daytime TV. I dumped the mysterious package and my shopping (biscuits, milk and toilet roll, which summed up everything you needed to know about my life) and put the kettle on.

Cup of tea in one hand, the other occupied by the precariously balanced package, mobile phone and biscuits, I headed for the sofa. I put the tea down and picked up the TV remote, already knowing exactly what I was going to watch but lying to myself about it. I flicked the TV on.

It was one of those morning magazine programmes. You know the kind: fashion, health, 'soft' news items, cookery, celebrity interviews...

"Top o' the morning to you!" The cheery Irish host, who always had a twinkle in his eye, a slight bulge in his trousers and a vacant but beautiful female host next to him, greeted the audience with his trademark cheeky grin. He was one of those people who was a bit of a tosser but you kind of couldn't help liking him. He KNEW he was a tosser, which somehow made all the difference. "And on the Top Of The Morning sofa today we have award winning crime novelist Joel Quigley..." I could feel my teeth involuntarily gritting. "...Talking about his new autobiography, 'In My Own Words'."

In his own words? That made a fucking change.

My phone rang, making me jump and drop the teetering pile of stuff in my hand. I scrabbled for the phone and looked at the number: Susie. Crap. Susie's probably my best friend – we've known each other for years – but she's also my agent, which can sometimes be a bit stressful. I took a deep breath and answered.

"Susie! How's it going?"

"I'm fine. I've just run out of things to read..."

Subtle.

"Well, you'll be pleased to know that I've been writing this morning," I reassured her, cheerfully. I declined to tell her that I'd deleted everything afterwards, but hey. honesty isn't always the best policy, and there was no sense in worrying her.

"Hmmm..." she said suspiciously. "You do know that

updating your status on Facebook doesn't count as 'writing', don't you?"

"Of course it does!" I cried. "Not that I've been on it this morning. Much. I don't know why you have such a downer on social media anyway. It's a great way to keep in touch with my readers –"

"To over-share things with them –"

"I don't over-share! Much. It's a great tool."

"You're a great –"

I ignored her. "If the likes of Charles Dickens was alive now, he'd totally be on Twitter. You know he used to publish his novels in serial form, in his magazine? If he was alive now, he'd be sending them out into the world in batches of 280 characters."

"It's not exactly great literature though, is it?" she sighed.

"No," I said. "It's Twitterature."

She groaned, even though it was probably one of my better jokes.

My attention drifted away from the conversation and onto the TV screen. Award winning crime novelist, borderline narcissist and unfaithful ex-husband Joel Quigley sat on the TV sofa and smiled his most charming smile at the blonde female host opposite him, who giggled coquettishly. Bastard. He could do everyone a favour and stop being so bloody young and sexy and handsome...

The female presenter smiled, showing her perfect teeth, and spoke. "The book of course covers a turbulent period of your life, detailing not just your awards and success, but also the end of your marriage to fellow crime writer Annabelle Tyson."

I was betting it didn't cover him screwing the barmaid at our local pub.

"Yes," said Joel the bastard unfaithful ex-husband, looking sad and sincere. If I gritted my teeth any more I'd wear them down to the gums. "It was a difficult decision to leave Bella. As a much older woman she taught me a lot about life – "

"You utter bloody cock!" I shouted at the TV. "'Much older woman'? And I left you, you arrogant – "

"Bella! Bella!" Susie's voice shrieked in my ear. I calmed down, holding the phone away from my head.

"Sorry, Suze, I couldn't help myself. That git's on the telly –"

"I know, you idiot. Why do you think I chose this moment to ring you?"

I felt even more guilty. My best friend had rung to save me from myself. I really didn't deserve her.

"I can't help it," I said. "It's like picking at a scab. You know it's just going to make it bleed again, but you have to do it."

She sighed. "Well, when you've finished picking your scabs – " I could hear the slight shudder of disgust in her voice – " how about meeting me for lunch? Lorenzo's, tomorrow at 1?"

Tomorrow at 1? That gave me – I looked at the clock – roughly twenty six hours to finish my new book, if I didn't sleep, eat, go to the toilet...I'd have to START my new book first, of course, but it was entirely doable...

"Sounds great!" I said. "See you then!"

I did try. I really did. I turned the TV off the minute I put the phone down on Susie. I sat and drank my tea, musing over the plot ideas I'd come up with on my walk to and from the corner shop (which didn't take very long), thoughtfully making my way through half a packet of biscuits before I realised what I was doing and stopped.

As I pushed the packet away from me in disgust, something caught my eye. The mysterious package. I really couldn't remember ordering anything. I picked it up and looked at the postmark: Venice. Curiosity well and truly piqued, I ripped the tape off and tore into the brown paper wrapping.

Inside was a book. *Ghosts, Ghouls and Mysterious Spirits: the Dark History of Italy's Flooded City* by one Francesca Vialli. I DEFINITELY hadn't ordered it, but I liked the sound of it. Venice was on my bucket list, one of those places I really wanted to see but just hadn't got round to yet. The bastard unfaithful ex-husband had promised to take me there on our tenth wedding anniversary, more than likely in the knowledge that his money was safe, since it was doubtful we'd make it that far, given his propensity for bonking barmaids.

I opened the book and started to read.

That night I dreamt I was in Venice. I sat in a gondola, hand trailing in the dark waters of the lagoon as a skeletal figure, clad in the traditional stripy t-shirt and red sash, swept us past crumbling palazzos, under bridges and along shadowy canals, twisting our way through the city until I was hopelessly lost in her.

The soft lapping of the waves lulled me into a trance. I gazed up at the lights in the windows of the once-grand houses lining the waterways, mysterious silhouettes dancing and laughing, living and loving in the candlelit warmth as I shivered outside, floating wraith-like along the canal.

The cold water numbed my submerged hand. I didn't notice the sea-stained fingers wrapping themselves around mine until they tugged at me with shocking strength, waking me from my stupor. I tried to pull my hand away but their grip grew tighter, trying to tug me over the side. I grabbed the smooth polished wood of the boat with my other hand, but it was slippery, sea-salt-slicked under my skin.

With growing terror I wedged my feet against the side of the madly rocking gondola, listening to the skeleton gondolier serenade me with its mocking laughter.

And then it stopped. I pulled my icy cold hand out of the water and clutched it to my chest, trying to massage some warmth and life back into it.

Gingerly, I peered over the side of the boat. My reflection – pale skin, messy hair, wide eyes – peered back. I laughed uneasily and reached out a hand to shatter that ghostly face –

- and jumped awake, heart pounding, drenched in cold sweat. Shakily I reached out a hand to reassure myself that my bed hadn't been surrounded by a deep, dark lagoon while I slept, then lay on my back and stared at the ceiling until sleep finally re-claimed me.

CHAPTER TWO

I was late for my lunch with Susie. I always am. Lorenzo's is our favourite restaurant; it's our designated lunch spot and I've even done a Norma No-Mates and eaten there alone - and yet I still never manage to arrive on time. It's only a fifteen minute walk from my house, so of course I faff about at home getting ready, thinking I've got loads of time, and before I know it I've only got five minutes to get there.

Susie looked at her watch pointedly as I burst in and made my way to our usual table.

"Yes, I know, I'm late, sorry!" I panted, slipping into a chair. "Traffic was terrible."

"You walked! You only live round the corner. "

I grinned and reached for the wine glass in front of her. "What's that, in your glass?"

She frowned. "There's nothing in my glass –"

"Ah ha! That's your problem right there, then." She laughed as I looked round for a waiter.

"It's lunch time! Are you trying to get me drunk?"

"Don't worry, my intentions are honourable. You're not my type. No penis."

"Oh, so you do still have a type then?" said Susie. "It's been a while..."

"You know I don't go in for casual stuff," I said, waving over to the bar. "Especially these days. I'm getting too old to mess around. When I fall for a bloke, it's hard and fast –"

She sniggered. I treated her with the contempt she deserved.

"You know what I mean! It's all or nothing, bolt-from-the-blue time." I managed to attract the young waiter's attention and we both watched him make his way over to the table.

"Now THAT'S any hot blooded woman's type," murmured Susie appreciatively, admiring his muscular frame and short blonde hair.

"You are such a cougar!" I said, shaking my head. "Poor Guy."

"Poor Guy my arse! He knows I'd never cheat on him," she said. "Just because I'm on a diet it doesn't mean I can't study the menu. But there's nothing stopping you going for it –"

"No, just my self respect! I've got stuff in the freezer older than he is."

We ordered a cheeky bottle of red and a seafood risotto and set about the tricky task of avoiding talking about my work, or lack there of. But of course in the end we had to.

"So, you said you'd been writing..." Susie spoke as if on eggshells.

"Yes, that's why I was late. I was so into Chapter 13..."

"Really?!"

"No, not really."

"I thought you were writing about the Transplant Killer?"

"The doctor who goes around killing people for their organs? Yeah, I was but my heart wasn't in it."

"Or there was the other idea you told Guy about –"

'The one who kills politicians by shoving fireworks up their arse? That fizzled out."

"Oh. We both really liked that one..."

"Well, I haven't written either of those or anything else. So if the purpose of lunch was to discuss my book we'd better cancel the food, because it's not going to be a very long discussion."

She looked at me with a surprisingly angry look on her face.

"Do you think that's the only reason I wanted to see you? To forcibly drag another bestseller out of you?"

"Well, that's your job –"

"For god's sake, Bella! I've been your agent so long now that we're practically bloody family. You're not 'my job', you're my friend and I'm worried about you."

I hung my head in shame, which made it really difficult to knock back my glass of wine but I managed somehow.

"I am trying to write –"

"I don't CARE about the writing!" she spluttered. "I care about you! You've shut yourself away, you never go anywhere –"

"I do!" I protested. "I went to – well, I went to Ikea last week."

"That's not what I mean and you know it. You used to socialise. How many people did you talk to last week? Not on the phone, face to face?"

"Including the staff at Ikea? None. Actually I said hello to the postman –"

The waiter brought our food to the table. It looked and smelt delicious but neither of us felt hungry now. I pushed a disconsolate-looking langoustine around my plate as Susie drained her glass.

"I'm in a rut," I said, finally.

"No shit."

"But I've got a plan." I hadn't had a plan up to that moment, but it suddenly became very clear to me what I had to do. "That's why I was late."

I reached into my bag and pulled out the book. Susie took it and looked at the front page, puzzled.

"Ghosts, Ghouls and Mysterious Spirits? What the sweet Jesus is this?"

"Inspiration." I grabbed the book back and flicked through it. "Someone sent me this yesterday and I've read the whole thing already. It's great! It's such a wonderful, macabre setting. This is what I need to write. A supernatural crime story!"

"Your fans want more DCI Fletcher –"

"Well they're not getting any more. I mean it, Susie, I think this is why I'm stuck. I'm done with the past. I'm done with DCI Fletcher and her ridiculous crush on Viktor. I mean, we're five books in, if they haven't got it on by now then it's not happening, is it? I think Viktor's gay."

Susie held up a hand to silence me. "Did you hear that? That was the sound of your female readers' hearts breaking. Not Viktor!"

"All right, maybe SHE'S gay then. I'm done with the both of them. I'm done with London, and most of all I'm done with Joel, the barmaid-shagging, talentless himbo!"

I flung my arms out wide to emphasise just how much I was over the bastard unfaithful ex-husband. Luckily the waiter was passing and he managed to save the flying wine glass. He handed it back to me with a grin.

"Thank you," I said, momentarily losing my stride.

"So you're going to write a ghost story?" asked Susie. "And set it in Venice?"

"Not just setting it there," I said. "I'm writing it there. The woman who sent me the book – she's the author, Francesca – well, she's offered me the use of her apartment for a few months if I want it -"

"Whoa whoa whoa!" Susie interrupted. "Who is this woman?"

"I TOLD you, she wrote the book. She's an Italian grandma who writes ghost stories and is a big fan of mine and who has a lovely big empty apartment five minutes walk from San Marco..."

Susie frowned. "How did she get your address? This didn't come through the office."

"I dunno. She's a writer, not a stalker. Whatever. She's going to visit her daughter and her new baby in Australia so her apartment –"

"What, are you bloody pen pals now or something?"

"There was a letter in with the book. I just emailed her to say thank you, I haven't said I'm going or anything yet, but - I want a change of scenery, Suze! I need to get away!"

"Then go to Venice, but don't stay in some random crazed fan's apartment for god's sake! You don't know who this Francesca is. She might be planning to turn you into ravioli. Treat yourself, stay at the Cipriani. Do a Hemingway, drink Bellinis at Harry's bar and shag unsuitable Italians –"

"I don't want to do a Hemingway! I want to live like a native. I

17

want to buy fish at the Rialto market and drink my morning espresso at a little café, watching the world go by..."

Susie rolled her eyes. "While eating a Cornetto and being serenaded by a gondolier, I suppose."

A brief image of my dream from the night before flashed into my mind, sending a chill up my spine. I mentally shook it off and laughed.

"Well you can hardly go to Venice and NOT go in a gondola, can you?"

Susie sighed. "You've made your mind up, haven't you?"

"Yes."

She poured us both another glass of wine and lifted hers in a toast.

"I can't stop you, and to be honest I don't know that I should anyway. So here's a toast. Here's to being spontaneous and reckless and doing whatever the hell it is you need to do to get you back to being yourself again."

I lifted my glass and smiled at her. "To Venice."

The rest of the week flew by. It felt so good to have something to look forward to again, rather than just a deadline I knew I wasn't going to hit, looming over the horizon.

I emailed Francesca, whose English was fortunately much better than my Italian, and arranged to pick up the keys to her apartment from an upstairs neighbour as she was already in Australia. Susie nagged at me to ask her how she'd got hold of my address – I haven't been listed in any phone book since the DCI Fletcher books took off – but I couldn't work out a way to do that without sounding rude, and besides, I didn't really care; I just wanted to be in Venice.

And then it was simply a matter of packing. I chucked a few things into my suitcase, then took one look at the rest of my wardrobe and decided I hated all of it. I was going to Italy, one of the most stylish places in the known universe; I couldn't spend the whole time there in my usual jeans and trainers. I decided I was going to become a new woman in Venice; I was going to buy lots of classic, stylish pieces and get myself one of these 'capsule wardrobe' things the women's magazines always talk about: a few beautifully tailored key pieces that go with anything, a little black dress, accessorised with a casually flung-on scarf.... I go through these phases and they usually last a couple of weeks, then I get sick of dressing like a grown up and brushing my hair every day, and go back to my jeans. But not this time! Venice was going to work its magic on my ENTIRE LIFE, not just on my writing.

The morning of my flight – my escape – arrived. Finally. I packed my laptop and checked that I'd saved my boarding pass onto my phone for the four hundredth time (I love technology but I don't altogether trust it). I handed over my house keys to Susie's assistant, Jennifer, who was house sitting for me, took one last look around and jumped in the taxi.

I had no idea how long I'd be away for; Francesca was staying in Australia indefinitely, and I intended to stay in her apartment for as long as it took to write at least the first draft of my new novel. But bearing in mind I didn't yet know what it was going to be about, that could be a very long time indeed...

From the back seat of the taxi I watched my house disappear from view as we turned out of my road, and I had the strangest feeling that I wouldn't be back.

CHAPTER THREE

The flight to Venice only takes a couple of hours and I managed to fidget with anxious excitement the whole way. By the time we landed at Marco Polo airport the man sitting next to me looked like he wanted to strangle me and frankly, I couldn't blame him; I wanted to strangle me too. *Calm down for Christ's sake!* I told myself. But I couldn't.

It's a fair walk from the airport to the ferry terminal, but luckily I only had a small suitcase to drag along, nipping at my heels and bashing into other travellers' legs like a badly trained puppy. The smell of the sea, which has always had a calming effect on me, only served to heighten my excitement further, and I was practically skipping by the time I reached the jetty where my water taxi was waiting.

I relaxed on the back seat of the speedboat, watching locals and tourists queuing for the ferries slowly making their way between the mainland and the islands in the lagoon, and slipped on my new sunglasses as the driver navigated the narrow channel out into the sea. In my head, I looked just like Audrey Hepburn as Holly Golightly; but then he opened the throttle and we were away, hair flying around my face and sea spray in my eyes, more of a dog's breakfast than one at Tiffany's.

I didn't care. I couldn't wipe the massive grin from my face as we tore through the waves, then turned into the Grand Canal and made our way slightly more sedately past the faded but still beautiful facades of grand palazzos, under bridges and in and out of the water buses plying their trade up and down the watery thoroughfare. By the time we reached the Rialto Bridge – the one everybody recognises – I was done for. Completely smitten. All the photographs I'd ever seen of this place, all the travelogues and tourist guides and the more in-depth research I'd done in the last week, none of it had prepared me for this. I watched the passing scenery in stupefied awe, that massive grin growing bigger and bigger until I thought it would split my face in two, drinking in the sights, the sounds, the SMELLS of Venice. Everybody I'd spoken to (none of whom had ever actually been there) had warned me that Venice smelt. They'd all nodded wisely and murmured cautionary words about 'the drains', but they were talking shit. Literally. Venice smelt WONDERFUL to my London-abused nostrils; it smelt of the sea, salt-crusted on the boats and jetties and walkways, hell, on the people themselves. But even more than that, it smelt of food; seafood, fresh from the lagoon that morning, creamy risottos, pasta slicked with rich concoctions of tomato and cheese and basil and olive oil, every flavour of gelato you could imagine (along with others you couldn't), all mingled with the scent of coffee drifting out of the cafés lining the canal.

HEAVEN! God I was hungry. I couldn't wait to unpack and get my Eat Pray Love on.

The water taxi driver smiled at my obvious instant infatuation with his city – I realised later that he'd taken me the long way round, the scenic route, just to make me fall in love with the place – and turned the boat down a side canal, the Rio de l'Barcaroli, just as the pillars of the Doges Palace and the famous square tower of Piazza San Marco came into view. We squeezed past a row of gondolas waiting outside the Bauer Palazzo – they were in for a busy day, going by the long queue of tourists – and the driver waved his arm towards the square. "Prada, Chanel, nice shops!" he said. I wasn't sure if he'd heard my inner monologue about the capsule wardrobe or just thought I was badly dressed.

We slowly passed the crowd making their way over the bridge and carried on further down the canal. It was suddenly deserted, almost eerily so after the madness that lay just behind us. Here, the hotels lining the waterway gave waay to less ostentatious – but all the more beautiful for it – residential houses, their once colourful paintwork faded by the sea and the passage of time, wrought iron balconies slowly rusting from black to orange. Wooden shutters were flung wide to let the light and air into musty rooms while the faint sound of chatter, laughter among friends, reached me from some distant locanda, just serving to make the houses around me feel even emptier.

I shivered for a moment, suddenly reminded of the dream I'd almost forgotten. But the next minute the boat pulled over at stone steps leading into a tiny square, bathed in a ray of afternoon sunlight from a narrow passageway between the crowded buildings.

"Is here!" cried the driver, cheerily, and I leapt up, making the boat rock. He helped me out of the boat, lifted the suitcase out for me and with a wave, left me to it.

I looked around. I knew which house I HOPED it would be – the one with the little Juliet balcony overlooking the canal – and I did a little jig when I saw that it was indeed Francesca's apartment. If I couldn't write here, well then –

I didn't want to finish that sentence in case it was true.

I tried the front door – Francesca's neighbour knew what plane I was going to be on, so I thought she might have left it unlocked in preparation – but it stayed firmly shut, so I turned to the peeling blue green paint of the door next to it, and knocked loudly.

I almost peed my pants when the door was opened within SECONDS by an elderly woman, wearing massive dark glasses and a ridiculously floppy hat. She must've been lurking in the hallway, waiting for me to knock.

"Holy shit!" I yelped.

"Si?" said the woman, peering at me. I couldn't see her eyes through those dark lenses but I could tell she was peering at me short-sightedly.

"Buongiorno!" I said, sounding terribly English. I'm not great at other languages anyway, but I never know whether or not I should attempt the accent, in case it sounds like I'm taking the piss. Da pasta justa like a Mama used to a maker! That kind of thing. Anyway –

"Francesca said I should get the keys from you?" I said, speakng VERY LOUDLY AND SLOWLY because of course that's how you speak to foreigners, whilst miming using a key to unlock a door. God knows what I looked like, but she got the idea.

"Si, si, 'keys'!" she said, reaching behind her and passing them out to me.

"Grazie –" I began, and then stopped as she shut the door in my face. Welcome to Venice.

Never mind! Weird grumpy neighbours notwithstanding, I was already hooked on the place and I couldn't wait to see what my home for the next however-many months looked like from the inside. I picked up my case, opened the door and stepped over the threshold.

CHAPTER FOUR

It was cool and dark inside after the glaring sunlight of the square. I walked through the open plan living area to the French doors at the far wall, where a tiny chink of sunshine squeezed in through a gap in a wooden shutter. I opened the doors, flung the shutters open wide and stepped out onto the tiny balcony.

Sensory overload. The smell of the sea, the beauty of the sun-flecked ripples in the water below and the sudden heat all hit me at once, with such intensity that for a moment all I could do was clutch onto the iron railing and wait for it to pass. Wow. I didn't get THAT looking out the window of my house in Wimbledon. Why the hell did I live in London? From now on I was only ever going to live by the sea.

I felt suddenly light and carefree. Bollocks to the bastard unfaithful ex-husband! I should've done this years ago. Straight after finding him in the toilets with that bimbo at the Smoking Gun awards in 2013, actually. I should never have given him a second – then a third – chance, I should've kicked him out, sold the house and moved here. I should've said *stuff this for a game of soldiers* and gone off to have adventures. Ah well. Better late than never.

"Bloody hell, I love this place...!" I sang to myself, surprising a passing gondolier and his boat full of Japanese tourists.

"Ciao, signore!" I called out, waving happily. He smiled and waved his hat at me in salutation, then burst into song – I had no idea what he was singing, it was in Italian (obviously) but I recognised the tune as being something operatic. The tourists gawped at me and I giggled as I went back inside.

The rest of the apartment was nice enough, but I knew that I would be spending most of my time at the little wooden desk where Francesca had, no doubt, written the book that had lured me there. I dragged it across the floor so that it sat in the window; now it had the perfect, inspiring view. I unpacked my laptop and sat it on the desk, ready for action, but there was no way I was going to start writing yet.

I wanted to explore.

I reached out to close the shutters again and stopped; I could hear the elderly neighbour upstairs, talking very loudly and heatedly on the telephone. It sounded like she was having a massive argument with someone, but in my short time there I'd already spotted that Italians can get very loud and excitable when they're deep in conversation, so maybe that's all it was. Being a writer, I'm inquisitive (*nosey*) and observant (*an eavesdropper*) and I cursed the fact that I couldn't speak Italian and work out what she was saying. Maybe I'd pick up some of the lingo while I was there.

I closed the French doors and picked up a guidebook.

I locked the street door behind me and looked around, getting my bearings. The other thing everybody tells you about Venice, apart from the smelly drains, is that you're bound to get lost at some point. But being possessed of a stout heart, a good sense of direction and a bloody-minded nature, I was determined to prove them all wrong.

I followed the narrow passageway ahead of me onto the Calle Largo XXII Marzo, coming out dead opposite the Gucci shop. That was handy. *Capsule wardrobe here I come,* I thought; but judging by the wonderful food aromas wafting my way, all of these well tailored, classic pieces I was planning on buying would have to have elasticated waists. I wondered how much a pair of Gucci jogging bottoms would cost.

I wasn't in the mood for shopping right now anyway, I was in the mood for romance, adventure, culture – but mostly some of that hazelnut gelato...

Cone in hand, I walked across the bridge I'd earlier floated under, still packed with tourists waiting for their turn on a gondola, and onwards towards Piazza San Marco. The streets were narrow, lined with the 'nice shops' the taxi driver had pointed out to me – Louis Vuitton, Sisley, Chanel – I could feel my credit card straining at its leash. Onwards. Ahead of me I could see a colonnade of grey stone pillars, a bright and exciting glimpse of the square beyond visible through the arches.

I quickened my pace, leaving the claustrophobic, people-packed street behind me and stepping out into the open air of Saint Mark's Square. I could breathe freely in the sudden sunshine again.

I stopped and looked around me. Ahead, the square stone bell tower of San Marco thrust its way above the crowd queuing outside the basilica. Next to me, under the colonnade that ran around three sides of the square, shops full of blown glass and expensive but slightly tacky souvenirs led on towards the famous Caffe Florian which, according to my guide book, was a popular hangout back in the day for the likes of Casanova (when he wasn't, ahem, 'otherwise occupied' or in prison) and later, Lord Byron and Charles Dickens.

I followed in their literary footsteps and went inside, marvelling at the opulent gilding and incredible frescoes that decorated every surface. And then came straight back out and sat at an outside table, because quite frankly, wonderful as it was, that amount of gilding in one place set my teeth on edge and gave me a migraine.

I sipped at a café latte and watched the world go by, and it struck me again how carefree I felt. It felt like I was playing hooky from real life.

I finished my coffee and strolled on, listening to the tourists milling around under the clock tower, tour guides counting heads and handing out leaflets and audio guides, leading their charges off with umbrellas or flags held aloft. So many different languages and accents. The whole world had come to Venice, but only on a day trip; the cruise liners emptying their human cargo in the morning then taking them back when the tide was high.

I wandered along the Riva degli Schiavoni, the sea front walk that passed the Doges Palace and its Bridge of Sighs, row upon row of gondolas and ferries and day trip boats lining the quay. I passed the tourist hordes and the migrant workers flogging dodgy plastic tat on the bridges – selfie sticks and badly made carnival masks. I found a table at a quiet sea front restaurant, just opening for the evening, and parked my by-now aching feet while I watched the sun set over the lagoon.

I got back to the apartment about 9pm, after stopping at a small convenience store to buy tea bags and milk. As great as the restaurants and cafes were, I reminded myself that I was supposed to be living like a local, and that meant shopping and cooking rather than eating out for every meal. Forget the Gucci shop; tomorrow I'd track down the nearest supermarket.

I made a cup of tea and put the TV on, flicking through the channels until I found an old American movie I'd already seen a dozen times dubbed into Italian, and sat back, thinking over the events of the day. I came to several conclusions, which I jotted down in the new notebook I'd bought especially for this trip (writers love stationery and will use any excuse to buy a new notebook):

1. *I BLOODY LOVE THIS PLACE! No cars/more people walking about = much more civilised than London*
2. *I still have NO FUCKING IDEA what my book is going to be about – I need to explore the city first – gondola ride? Day trip to the other islands? Do the tourist thing?!*
3. *This place is too romantic to be single...*

I stared at the last one and shook my head in disgust at myself, then stopped as something on the desk across the room – the one I'd moved that afternoon – caught my eye. A piece of paper sat under a Murano glass paperweight that I'd admired earlier.

It was a note from Francesca, folded over with another piece of paper inside. I don't know how I'd missed that before, but maybe I'd been just too excited to pay any attention to it.

Ciao Bella (it read),

Welcome to Venezia! I hope my apartment suits you and you have everything you need.

(Then a list of instructions on operating the water heater, directions to the local supermarket, that sort of thing)

I hope you will enjoy all the sights that Venice has to offer. As a welcome gift, I have booked you a gondola tour for your first day – it is a unique way to see the back 'streets' of the city. The details are on the email enclosed.

I scanned the email print out but it was (of course) all in Italian. I could however make out the when (tomorrow morning at 10.30) and the where (Campiello Traghetto, about 10 minutes walk away). The spectre of the skeletal gondolier from my dream rose into my mind again but I pushed it away easily; now I was actually here, Venice held no fears for me – I already loved it too much to be afraid of it. My brief walk around the city had been enough to make me feel at home. And a gondola ride – although a complete tourist cliché – WAS on my to do list; you couldn't come to Venice and not go on a gondola.

Exhausted but excited about the day ahead of me tomorrow, I finished my tea and went to bed. I lay on my back, watching the reflections of the moonlit canal dance on my ceiling, and listened to the gentle lapping of the water until I drifted off to sleep.

CHAPTER FIVE

I woke early, leaping out of bed and flinging the bedroom window open wide. A narrow boat carrying boxes of fruit and vegetables chugged past, the driver raising his hand in greeting.

I smiled up at the sky and resolved to *carpe* the shit out of this *diem*.

Half an hour later I was out of the house. I wandered towards Campiello Traghetto, although I was far too early for my gondola trip, then carried on walking through the winding streets until I came across another square where several cafes were open for breakfast.

I picked one at random and sat outside, trying to decipher the menu. At the next table, a man – middle aged, nice looking in a dependable kind of way, drained his coffee and reached over to pick up a bag. As he straightened up, our eyes met – not in a fireworks exploding, violins playing kind of way, but more *oh shit I just made eye contact with a stranger*. He started in surprise and I looked away, embarrassed.

You know when you order yourself not to look back again – but you really want to know if they're still looking at you, and you just can't help but turn your head? I looked round again to see him studying me carefully. We both turned away in a hurry, and I narrowly avoided head butting the waitress who had just appeared and was placing a jug of water on the table.

I ordered an espresso and a croissant, cheeks burning, and sat back, studiously looking at the menu, the buildings on the other side of the square, anything other than him.

"I hope you like it strong." I looked up and he was standing next to my table, smiling shyly and clutching his bag to his chest. I smiled up at him. He suddenly looked horrified. "The coffee! I meant – oh god. Sorry. You are - English, aren't you?"

"Is it that obvious?' I laughed.

"It is to me. But that might be because I am too."

The waitress brought my breakfast. He gestured to the coffee.

"I hope you like strong coffee. That's what I meant before. The espresso here has a real kick to it."

I picked up the tiny cup gingerly. "I like my coffee how I like my men."

He looked slightly disappointed. "Ah, yes, I've heard that one. Hot, strong and – "

"Warm, sweet and milky, actually," I said. He laughed.

"Definitely English. Well, enjoy your breakfast. It was nice meeting you."

"And you."

And then he was gone, trotting off briskly across the square. I resolved to come back the next day for breakfast. Just in case... I sipped at the espresso and grimaced. But I'd order a latte tomorrow instead.

I had a wander around after breakfast, killing time before my boat trip, then headed back to the gondola office. But when I showed the gondolier the email Francesca had left me, he went off into a mad Italian rant that I had no chance of following. The gist of it was clear, however: no gondola ride.

I was just about to give up – I could always book for another day, or go and join the queue of tourists I'd passed yesterday – when I felt someone at my shoulder.

"Can I be of any assistance?"

It was Coffee Man, looking at me and the exasperated gondolier anxiously. I smiled gratefully.

"Oh yes please! My friend booked a gondola ride for me but there's some kind of problem. I don't know, I don't speak Italian and he doesn't speak English so we've been going round in circles for the last ten minutes..."

"Can I?" He held out his hand for the piece of paper and scanned it quickly. "Ah yes. It looks like your friend has printed out the wrong thing. This is her booking but it's not the actual ticket."

"Oh. Oh well, it doesn't matter, I'm happy to pay for a ticket –"

"No, no!" he said. "He's being pedantic. Give me a minute."

He took the gondolier to one side and started to talk to him in rapid, fluent (to my ears, anyway) Italian. I was impressed. His attention on the other man, I studied him more carefully.

I always study new people. Not just their appearance, but their mannerisms and funny little ways. It helps me come up with characters for my books. He wasn't particularly tall – 5'5", 5'6" I reckoned, comparing him with me (I'm 5'2) – not fat, but not skinny either (did he work out? more likely ran or cycled). Short dark hair, starting to grey a little at the sides. Nice smile. Friendly eyes. Not exactly hero material – too old for that – the hero's mentor, maybe? Or his dad. Hmmm.

Nice bum –

I looked up and blushed as I realised he'd spotted me checking out his, ahem, physical attributes. He smiled at me.

"All sorted."

"Really?"

"Yes. Give him *un momento* and he'll be with you."

"Thank you so much! That's so kind of you to help me –"

"Not at all. We can't have you getting the wrong impression of our fair city on your first day, can we?"

"How did you know it's my first day?"

For a split second his smile seemed to falter. But it was back again so quickly that I may have been imagining it.

"Everyone does a gondola trip on their first day!"

I laughed. "Fair point. Did you?"

"Er – no, actually. I came here for work and I had to start more or less straight away. In fact I still haven't got round to doing one."

The gondolier came back and gestured towards the boat, speaking to Coffee Man.

"No, no –" he said.

"Is everything ok?" I asked.

"Yes, he wants us to get in the boat and I was just telling him I'm not coming – he thought we were together."

"Oh, right."

I stopped and looked at him for a moment. He really did have

34

a nice smile. I thought back to my list of observations from the night before.

1. *This place is too romantic to be single...*

Carpe diem. I swallowed hard.

"Look, I'm sure you're probably busy –"

"No, I had a meeting this morning but it got cancelled."

"Well, in that case, if you haven't been on a gondola before –" *Don't make me ask you, you know what I'm getting at* – "Would you like to join me?"

He looked surprised. "Join you?"

And now I feel like an idiot. "If you're busy that's fine –"

"No no no!" he burst out. "I'd love to! I mean, that would be really nice, if you're sure?"

The gondolier, who I was starting to suspect knew more English than he'd previously let on, watched us incredulously, shaking his head at these stupid repressed British people.

"Yes, I'm sure," I said, definitely.

"*Finalmente!*" the gondolier muttered under his breath. "You get on now, yes?"

We got on.

We settled down at the end of the gondola and Coffee Man turned to me, holding out his hand to shake.

"Will Carmichael," he said. I took his hand.

"Pleased to meet you. I'm Bella – Bella –" I hesitated, I don't know why; perhaps because I've been taken advantage of too many times once people know who I am. Once they know I'm rich and (I have to modestly admit) quite famous, in literary circles anyway. "Bella Jones."

Again, that slight faltering of the smile, then – "Bella! That's a very apt name for Italy."

"And everybody told me it was Italian men I had to look out for, not British ex-pats..."

He laughed. "That did come across as much smoother than I intended. I just meant it was Italian."

"Oh right!" I said, in mock indignation. He looked embarrassed.

"Not that you're not – I didn't mean –" He saw my smile and stopped with a rueful grin. "Shall I just stop talking?"

"That might be best..."

We lapsed into a companionable silence as the gondolier pushed away from the side. The gondola glided through the still water, then out into the choppier waves of the Grand Canal.

Will knew a lot about the history of Venice and as we rocked gently along he pointed out buildings and places of interest. He was good company after his initial shyness, warming to his subject and sharing his fondness for the city around us.

"How do you know so much about this place?" I asked him.

"Books. When I knew I was being seconded here I read up on it. The history of this place is fascinating. The Venetians were way ahead of the rest of Europe when it came to trading with other countries. They were master ship builders, you see..."

I smiled at his boyish enthusiasm.

"I'm sorry," he said. "I haven't spoken to many English people since I got here, and it's really nice to use my own language again."

"It's really nice to listen to you," I said. "You said you were seconded here. What do you do?"

Will spoke vaguely. "Oh, nothing interesting. I'm a consultant. I –"

"Consult?"

"Ha! Yes. How about you? How long are you on holiday for?"

"Oh, I'm not on holiday. I'm here because –" I hesitated again. When you tell people you're a writer, the first thing they ask is *'anything I might've read?'* Which is really bloody annoying when you're still yet to publish anything, and tricky when you've sold a ton of books and won awards but you're trying to be discreet about who you are. Oh well – "I'm a writer. I'm staying here while I write my next book."

"Oh I see."

I waited for the inevitable question about what I had written but it didn't come. *And relax.*

"Well, you couldn't have come to a more inspiring city! It's so romantic –" He looked mortified at what he'd just said and then hurtled on with the rest of the sentence – "and – and atmospheric. Have you heard about Poveglia? *L'isola della morte?*"

I recognised that name from a story in Francesca's book.

"Yes! I read a story about it. It was a hospital island, wasn't it?"

"Sort of. Way back in the 1700s the Venetians made every ship entering the lagoon stop there for 40 days. It was a quarantine station."

"Oh," I said, vaguely disappointed. "I thought it was where they sent plague sufferers to die?"

Will smiled grimly. "Well, yes. Two ships stopped at the island and turned out to be carrying the Black Death. It spread to the mainland, so they started to send anyone showing symptoms to Poveglia to try and contain it. Thousands of people died and were buried there. Some say that to this day the soil is mostly the ashes of the poor unfortunates sent there to die."

"Lovely. But wasn't there an actual hospital on the island as well?"

"Yes. That's where the story gets interesting. In the 1920s a mental institution was opened on Poveglia, run by a sadistic doctor who performed experiments on his patients. He eventually threw himself off the hospital's bell tower, driven mad by the ghosts of his victims."

I shuddered. "Oh that is brilliant! I love it." I laughed at the amused look on Will's face. "Sorry. I write murder mysteries and I quite fancy doing a supernatural one this time."

"Well you really did come to the right place, then."

I looked around at the passing scenery, and smiled.

"I hope so! I love it here already. From the minute we turned into the Grand Canal on the way in from the airport, I was hooked. It's just like all the photographs and paintings you've ever seen of Venice –"

"Only more so."

I laughed. "That's it! It's more Venice than I ever imagined."

The gondolier turned the boat back towards its mooring. We sat quietly, both wondering – well, I was at least – whether or not to make some kind of move.

The gondolier helped us both out and busied himself, tying up the gondola, while we stood and smiled at each other.

"Well, thank you for inviting me along –" Will said.

"Thank you for sorting it all out! And for being such a good tour guide."

He laughed. "Sorry, I talk too much when I get excited about things."

"No, it was great! I really enjoyed your company."

"Oh, good."

We stood and looked at each other. *Say something, for fuck's sake woman!*

"So – make sure you go to the Guggenheim, it's really worth it," said Will, shuffling his feet awkwardly.

"I will," I said. "I want to explore everywhere. "

"Good."

"Good."

Out of the corner of my eye I could see the gondolier grinning, highly amused.

"Well –" began Will.

"Poveglia!" I cried, seizing on an opportunity to keep him talking. "I want to go to Poveglia. Um – I don't suppose you know how to get there?"

He shook his head. "Thing is, it's private property and although the owner doesn't really mind people going there, the authorities discourage it."

"Why?"

"They think some of the more unsavoury locals go there to, well, do unsavoury things I suppose. And there's no ferry or anything; I had to charter a boat –"

"You've been there?"

"Yes," said Will, uncomfortably. "There's not really anything there, it's just got this atmosphere –"

"Where did you find the boat?"

"I wouldn't want you to get into trouble –"

"Trouble? That's settled, I'm DEFINITELY going. Please?" I looked up at him with my best puppy dog eyes. He laughed.

"All right! Here, give me that bit of paper and I'll write down the address of the boat yard. They might not want to take you though, as the police are trying to stop tourists going there..."

Will scribbled something down and handed me the bit of paper.

"Um, my phone number's on there as well, just in case you want another guided tour..."

I smiled broadly at him. "Thank you so much! I'm really glad we bumped into each other."

"Me too. It was lucky, wasn't it?" He looked at his watch. "I really have to go. I hope we bump into each other again."

"I have a feeling we will," I said.

I watched him go. As he reached the corner of the street, he turned and looked back, and seemed surprised that I was watching him. He shyly lifted a hand and waved, then hurried away. I sighed. He was sweet.

"*Gli inglese pazzi!*" murmured the gondolier, shaking his head again.

"Oh shut your face, gelato breath, what do you know?" I said, and wandered off.

CHAPTER SIX

I found a shady café table and sat down to sip at a cool drink and reflect on the morning's events. The gondola ride had been amazing, thanks to my new friend (I felt myself going all soft and girly at the thought of Will) and his knowledge of the city, and I really hoped that I'd get a chance to explore Venice some more with him, because he could really help me with my research. *Oh, right. We're calling it 'research' these days, are we?*

I drank some more of my ice-cold lemon granita. *Get a grip, woman.* It was this place! After two years of being single, I'd come to the conclusion that I didn't have a romantic bone in my entire body. And after less than 24 hours in Venice I was starting to feel like a giggly schoolgirl, all over some bloody 40-odd year old IT consultant with a nice smile and a public school accent. *He IS nice though...*

I shook my head to clear the sudden granita-induced brain freeze and took out the bit of paper. Will might have a nice smile, but he had terrible handwriting and I could only just make out the address he'd written down. I managed to decipher it and typed it into the Map app on my phone.

It was a 15 minute walk away...

---

25 minutes later (I got, not lost, more 'temporarily misplaced') I was standing outside a boatshed on the Fondamente Zattere. It looked like an old warehouse building, with a crane to hoist boats in and out of the water. An old man sat outside, dozing in the sunshine.

It didn't look that promising.

"Posso aiutarla, signora?"

I whirled round to see an extremely good looking young man – olive skinned, dark haired, bare-chested and muscular – holding a mobile phone, calling to me from a boat. *DING DONG! Oh stop it, woman, are you on heat or something?*

He spoke into his phone – *"É qui, ciao!"* – disconnected the call, and spoke again. "I can help you, signora?"

"I hope so –"

He grinned. *Not like that, you cocky bugger!*

"I want to go to Poveglia, I need to hire a boat. A friend said you might –"

He grinned again -- *god he's got perfect teeth* -- and shook his head. "No signora, *la polizia*, they don't like us going there. They say it's dangerous -"

"Good!" I said. "Danger is exactly what I'm after. When can you take me?"

"Ah, you want to look for ghosts, is that it? The ghost of old

Paolo, the doctor, huh? Hey, Papa!" He called to the old man, who woke up with a snort. *"Un altro cacciatore di fantasmi!"*

The old man cackled. I glared at them both stubbornly until they stopped laughing. The young man wiped his oily hands on a rag and climbed out onto the quayside.

"You're serious, yes? It will cost you a lot of money..."

"I have a lot of money," I said. He laughed again and stuck out his hand.

"I'm Gino."

"Bella." We shook hands.

"Ok Bella, crazy English lady, you have a deal. I'll take you to Poveglia."

"When?"

"Not today or tomorrow, but the day after that. Ok? But we leave early. I don't want *la polizia* to see us, we go before they wake up, yes?"

I could hear Gino's papa laughing as I walked away and wondered what I was letting myself in for.

That night I found myself a tiny restaurant in a quiet back street (my plan to live like a local and cook for myself wasn't gaining much traction thus far). I sat at a canal-side table, eating *spaghetti al nero di seppia* with just my trusty notebook for company.

My mind was racing with ideas. I just needed to wrangle them onto paper so I could see if they were any good. I talked to myself as I sucked up the slippery strands of pasta, gleaming with black squid ink, and picked up my pen.

Ok, so – a murder mystery with a hint of the supernatural. I was definitely in the right place for that, even before my visit to Poveglia. By day the main streets and squares of Venice bustled with tourists and the industries that had grown around them, but even then, if you ducked down a narrow side street or passageway it wasn't long before you found yourself in a completely different world, where the sun had a hard time finding its way in between the buildings and the locals kept to themselves and watched you with suspicion. At night, the winding roads all looked the same and it was easy to think you were on the right path home until it suddenly ended in a deep, black canal. There were dead ends everywhere, and gaps between the houses that were easy to miss (or just not marked on the tourist maps) that led who knew where. Even with my renowned sense of direction (renowned by me, anyway) I'd still got lost earlier in broad daylight, using a sat nav! It was definitely the sort of place where evil deeds could be done without raising too many eyebrows; where murderers and demons could turn tail and escape into the darkness, or into the water...

So, I had my genre, now I needed a protagonist. That was easy. I'll let you into a secret: every writer I know models their main character on themselves. Honestly. It might not be completely blatant – I mean, I don't think Tolkien was actually a hobbit or anything – but there'll be some aspect of the author, somewhere, in that character. I think it's a fairly safe bet that Jane Austen's mates read *Pride and Prejudice* and smiled knowingly to each other when they clapped eyes on Elizabeth Bennett.

Far be it from me to compare myself to Miss Austen, but all of my characters start life as me.

On the other side of the canal, my doppelganger appeared.

Sadly, ain't nobody got time for a slightly overweight, forty something divorced crime writer, so my main character – let's call her, hmmm, Ella – would have to be a younger, thinner, taller, prettier version of me. With more sass. And a quicker wit – the sort of woman who thinks of a brilliant comeback right there and then and not two hours later in the car on the way home.

My doppelganger elongated into a 5'6" size 8 blonde with silky hair and no wrinkles. I like to think she still looked a little bit like me. A tiny bit. Tiny, tiny -

Ok, Ella is a – what? detective? or maybe a crime writer??? (you see what I did there – like me) -- *I'll come back to that.*

Do we want a love interest? Hell yes.

Next to Ella, a Generic Love Interest (Male)/Hero appeared, looking an awful lot like Gino. Even down to the bare chest. Which gleamed. It was obviously well oiled.

I slurped my spaghetti and dripped black ink down my chin. Gino the Italian Stallion handsomely ran a hand through his luscious chestnut locks and tossed his head, handsomely, looking over at me and smiling. Handsomely. The light from a sudden brilliant shaft of moonlight that had conveniently appeared highlighted his (handsome) gleaming muscular form and glinted off his perfect white teeth with a 'ting!'. I shook my own head (not so handsomely); he was TOO godlike, too much of a hero, to the point where yes, I fancied him but at the same time I was slightly disappointed with myself for doing so. He was a complete and utter cliché and frankly, he had to go.

Not your archetypal Latin lover. How about tanned and blonde? Or pale and interesting with black hair?

Across the canal, my love interest grew and shrank and morphed and paled from a Californian surfer dude into an overgrown Emo. Now he looked like the lead in a teenage vampire movie. I shook my head again. This wasn't working; I just wasn't feeling it. He needed to be different.

The teenage vampire shrank into a malevolent-looking dwarf wearing a red coat, who looked at me in contempt and then said *'You have got to be fucking kidding me!'*

He disappeared with a 'POP!'

I sat back in my chair, wiping my chin with what I thought was a serviette but turned out to be the tablecloth, and closed my eyes. *Think, Bella.*

Not the hero – he's too old for that...the hero's dad? Hmmm...nice bum...

In my mind's eye, once again I saw Will turn round and smile at me by the gondola office, the sun behind him creating a halo around his (slightly thinning) hair. *Nice smile...*

I shook my head in disgust and snapped the notebook shut. Across the canal, Ella winked out of existence. I ordered another glass of prosecco and looked at the dessert menu. *Panna cotta di fragole* was the only thing that could save me now.

CHAPTER SEVEN

The day of my trip to Poveglia finally arrived. I'd spent the last 48 hours in a restless fugue, writing down random ideas, eating, listening to the elderly neighbour upstairs stomping around her flat and arguing on the phone, eating, visiting the Doges Palace (after which I could *not* stop singing a variety of popular music 'hits' to myself and replacing the word 'don't' with 'Doge'), eating, (*Doge you wish your girlfriend was hot like me*) taking a guided tour of Saint Mark's basilica (*Doge you forget about me*), and eating. (*Doge you want me, baby?*)

I visited the Gucci shop and the Chanel store and bought everything that fitted me (which wasn't much), taking it back to the apartment and hanging it in the closet without cutting the labels off – something telling me that it was probably destined to spend most of its life on a hanger while I went back to wearing jeans all the time. I found a very nice, very expensive but tasteful lingerie shop and spent a small fortune on underwear (knickers that were larger than I wanted to admit to and bras that involved

47

sheer lace, gorgeous silk and heavy duty scaffolding). I reckoned that it was about time the Bella Tyson Emporium of Erotic Delights re-opened for business and, as such, I ought to make sure the window dressing was enticing enough to lure prospective customers (*we all know who you're getting at!*) in through the doors...

I also spent HOURS agonising over whether or not I should call Will. It'd been a very long time since I'd dated anyone, and an even longer time since I'd rang someone to ask them out, and I didn't know what to do; did I want to risk looking too keen? Would that come across as desperate? Because I wasn't desperate, I just thought he was sweet and I was lonely and *oh god help me!!!*

In the end I decided that I *would* ring him, but only after my trip to Poveglia so that I'd have something to talk to him about.

The sun was up early and so was I. I made my way through streets that were still quiet, over the Ponte dell'Accademia and along the winding passageways to Gino's sea front boathouse. Sure enough, he was waiting for me on the boat, looking (if it were possible) even more ridiculously handsome than the first time I'd seen him.

He reached out a hand to help me onto the gently rocking boat and we set off.

It took about 40 minutes to reach Poveglia. Gino chatted happily all the way about his family, about how his grandfather had been a gondolier and then handed down the stripy top and the gondola to his (Gino's) uncle, who had made so much money at it that he'd retired early and bought a villa on Burano, one of the other islands in the lagoon.

"Maybe I should give up writing and become a gondolier," I laughed.

Gino looked horrified at the idea.

"Oh no, no lady gondoliers! Is not allowed! Besides, you can not just become a gondolier. It has to be in your blood – in your family. My *Nonno's* gondola is now run by my cousin, Cesare. He has a spot near the *Palazzo Gritti*. Plenty tourists want a gondola ride from there."

"The Gritti Palace? That's near Campiello Traghetto, isn't it? I think I may have met your cousin..."

"He is not like me," said Gino, shaking his head with a pitying look on his face. "My uncle's side of the family, they are not handsome like my father's side. They look like donkeys."

I laughed – poor ugly Cesare! – and looked across the lagoon at the island that was rapidly getting closer. I've always loved going on boats, even as a child when we used to get the ferry from Portsmouth to the Isle of Wight; I looked forward to the journey just as much as the actual holiday. There's something about the smell of the sea and the wind in my hair that always gets my pulse racing. It's a far more romantic way to travel than getting in a car or on a plane; you're trusting the elements to get you where you want to go, all the time knowing that you can never control the sea or the wind and that at any time they could blow you off course, sending you spiralling into an unplanned adventure, shipwrecking you on some distant shore...or on the Isle of Wight.

I don't know if it's because I'm a writer or just a daydreamer, but I do come up with some complete rubbish sometimes. I shook my head to clear it.

Gino carefully steered the boat into a canal which split the island into two. Both sides of the channel were overgrown in a tangle of bushes and trees. It was eerily quiet apart from the sound of the boat's engine, which at this slow speed had faded from a hearty roar to a dull chug. I couldn't even hear any birds.

Gino noticed my anxious face and smiled. "Don't worry, we moor down here so we're out of sight of any *polizia*," he said, and for the first time I realised that I was on a boat in the middle of a deserted lagoon with a man I didn't actually know. And no one knew I was here. *Fuck fuck fuuuck...*

We floated under a low bridge and moored next to some stone steps. Above us loomed the stone walls of the old hospital, moss covered and crumbling as Nature reclaimed the island. Gino leapt out of the boat and tied it up, then reached out a hand to pull me out.

I looked around. The jetty and the pathway leading away from it looked disappointingly well maintained for an abandoned ghost island, apart from the pile of empty food wrappers and drink cans next to the steps. Gino picked them up with an angry exclamation.

"Some people are pigs!" he said, throwing the litter into the boat.

"I thought nobody came here?" I asked.

He shrugged. "Some people come here for fishing. Is a good spot for it, nice and quiet, away from the ferries. Just locals."

"And the 'ghosts' don't bother locals, I suppose?" I said, sceptically. I had the feeling I'd been duped – another gullible tourist paying over the odds to hire a boat to a deserted island full of nothing but the detritus from fishing trips and the odd rat. Gino laughed.

"Oh, they bother locals if we go onto the island," he said. "When I was 15, my friends and I dared each other to stay on the island one night. We were big men, yes? So brave."

"What happened?" I asked.

"We found out that we were not such brave big men after all."

I looked at his face to see if he was having me on, but the look in his eyes as he remembered made me take him seriously.

He laughed. "Crazy English, I thought you wanted danger? You want ghosts, yes? Well that –" he pointed to the distant bell tower, on the south of the island. "- that is where you will find your ghosts."

Hmmm. Did I REALLY want ghosts? Hell yeah. I shouldered the backpack I'd brought with me and steeled myself.

"Come on, then! Bring it on!" I said impetuously. He grinned and shook his head.

"Oh no, I stay here with the boat. I catch nice fish for lunch, I even cook it for you, yes? Included in the price."

Shit.

"Oh – ok..."

"It's fine, the ghosts, they can not hurt the living. Although old Doctor Paolo, he does like to push people around."

"What does that mean?"

"I mess with you. Just stories. You are fine in the daylight. Now go or it will be time to go back!"

Ok. I could do this. I took a deep breath and headed away from the boat.

I climbed up the stone steps and found myself on the southern side of the low bridge we'd come under. Across the bridge was an overgrown wasteland, where (Gino had told me) the local government had tried in the 1960s and '70s to grow fruit and vegetables. But after the discovery of mass graves, pits of crumbling plague corpses mingling with the thin soil of the island, the Venetians had gone off the idea of eating produce from Poveglia and the farmers had given up, grateful for an excuse to leave. According to Gino, some of whose huge extended family had been involved in the project, many of the farmers had hated working on the island. It wasn't that they were suggesting it was haunted, exactly, just that there was an oppressive atmosphere that left them feeling too uncomfortable to work there alone.

I turned southwards instead, heading towards the bell tower in the distance. I was soon lost in the wild forest of trees that had sprung up between the bridge and main buildings of the hospital, unchecked and unattended to, yet instead of making me feel more uneasy I started to relax. The sun was shining, and where it had been starting to get uncomfortably hot out on the boat, here the canopy of leaves filtered the sunlight into dappled shade, making it a much more pleasant temperature for a pasty-skinned British woman. And no forest is ever completely quiet. Away from the canal there were birds in the trees, singing happily and then skittering away at the unaccustomed sight of a human being. Rustling in the undergrowth suggested that they weren't the only living inhabitants of the island.

I turned into a grove of fruit trees. There were figs, apples and lemons, all ripening in the sun and destined to go uneaten; such a waste! I reached out to pluck a fig from a nearby tree and then stopped, remembering just what made the soil here so fertile. Hmm. They weren't ripe yet, anyway...

At the other end of the orchard were a couple of ruined buildings. I'd managed to veer off track and end up on the west side of the island, away from the tower, but the decaying stone and rusty wire fencing (complete with warning signs) looked so inviting...

I strode up to the fence before my nerve gave out. Someone – another ghost hunter, I guessed – had been here before and cut through the wire. I looked at the gap in the fence and hesitated.

If this was a horror movie I'd be shouting at the screen right now, I thought. "Don't go in there, you stupid bint!" I said out loud, trying to build up my courage.

Bint...bint...bint... There was an echo.

"Well of course there's a fucking echo!" I said out loud.

'king echo...'king echo...'king echo...

I gulped.

"Shut up Bella, you great eejit!"

Eejit...eejit...eejit...

I face-palmed in exasperation at my own stupidity and stepped through the gap in the fence before I completely lost it. Then it was only a couple more strides before I was in the hospital itself.

CHAPTER EIGHT

It didn't take long to realise that, although abandoned, the island wasn't without its visitors. As I entered what once had probably been quite a grand entrance hall, I spotted several years' worth of graffiti on the walls, most (but not all of it) in Italian. I was by no means the only ghost hunter to climb through that gap in the fence.

The remains of a staircase crumbled slowly into dust at the far end of the hall, under a large window which once would have let welcome light into the building but was now almost completely choked by ivy and jungle-like creepers. After the gentle warmth and sunlight of the forest, it felt dark and cold in here – much colder than it should have done, I thought. I looked around. On either side of me, corridors – now missing the whole wall along one side – led along the front of the building, with gaping doorways leading off into what I assumed would in the past have been wards or operating theatres. Maybe this was the place where Doctor Paolo had performed his cruel and unnecessary procedures on patients who had themselves been abandoned, by families fearing that their loved ones' madness would spread.

I shuddered, then gave myself a good talking to. It was just a ruined building.

I set off down a corridor, taking out the small torch I'd thankfully packed in my backpack. It was quiet in here, particularly after the joyful sounds of the woodland, with nothing but the quiet creak of the building settling into its foundations, and the soft patter of falling dust disturbed by my movements.

I stopped in a doorway and shone the torch around. What made this place all the more sinister was the huge amount of stuff that had been left behind – as if the occupants had all suddenly just vanished, rather than been moved to other hospitals when the facility was closed. Rusting bed frames were piled up in one corner, while the broken legs of rotting wooden chairs littered the floor nearby. More ivy and a thick, flowering vine tumbled in through the window, glass long gone. The skeletons of long dead institutional furniture cast eerie shadows in the beam of my torch, which trembled slightly in my cold fingers. It *was* just the cold making me shake, honestly...

I turned away then froze as a sound reached me from inside the room. *Holy fuckoly* I thought to myself. *What are you doing, still standing there? Run!* But I had to – HAD to – see what had caused the noise that made my blood run like ice water in my veins and my heart pump so fast I thought it might burst.

I slowly turned back and shone the light around the deserted hospital ward, picking out the bed frames, the dead chairs, the horribly vigorous ivy at the window - which rustled loudly and exploded in a shower of leaves as a large bird burst out of it and into the room. It squawked in panic as it tried desperately to fly back out the way it had come, its wings flapping manically as it flew round the room and then towards daylight – which was right behind me.

I shrieked and fled from the room, along the corridor, out of the building and back through the fence, as if the devil himself was after me, and I didn't stop until I was back in the grove of fruit trees and heading towards the bell tower again.

I slumped against a tree for a moment to get my breath back, and took out a bottle of water. Two minutes later I was back in control of my heart rate (just about) and starting to feel like an idiot. Still clutching the bottle, I walked on towards the next lot of hospital buildings.

This wing of the institution was slightly better preserved; at some point in recent history the trees and bushes had been trimmed away and, although they were starting to creep back into the buildings, they still had a way to go before they completely took over. I took a deep breath –*she's back in the game!* – and entered the nearest doorway.

Like the other building, it was dark and cold, but there was no graffiti here; I got the feeling that no one had wanted to linger there long enough to spray anything. There were fewer furniture remains, but what was there looked all the more sinister for it; a small metal bed frame against one wall, next to an unidentifiable piece of machinery covered in rusting dials and switches. Had they performed electric shock therapy here? I felt a sudden deep sorrow for the poor souls who had been left here, probably by well-meaning relatives who thought they were providing them with the best care they could, only to have them suffer at the hands of a physician who was madder than they were.

I moved on to the next room, suddenly feeling icy fingers

prickling at my scalp. Was I being watched? I gripped the plastic water bottle tighter. I could feel someone – something – observing me, I knew it. I quietly slunk out of the room, keeping close to the wall, and now I thought I could hear breathing. *Ghosts don't breathe* I told myself, which maybe should've made me feel better, except that I remembered Gino's words: ghosts can't hurt the living. *No, but the living can.*

I inched my way along the wall, heading for another doorway out into a sunlit courtyard (why I should be any safer out there I didn't know, but I sure as hell wasn't staying inside!). I clutched the water bottle, raising it in my hand like a weapon. A puny one, but a weapon nonetheless. Almost there...another couple of inches...

And then Will appeared in the doorway. I screamed and (I'm not ashamed to say) a little bit of wee came out. My pelvic floor muscles were just not used to this sort of stress.

"Jesus Christ almighty, Bella!" he exclaimed, looking almost as shocked as I was. "What the bloody hell are you doing here?"

"I told you I was coming!" I said. "You gave me Gino's address, remember –"

"Yes, but I didn't think he'd actually bring you!" said Will, angrily. "He's been told to stop bringing tourists."

"I'm not a – anyway, what are YOU doing here?" I said.

He sighed and reached out to pluck the still-raised water bottle from my hand.

"What were you intending to do with that? Hydrate me?"

"You scared the shit out of me," I said. "This place..."

He took my hand and led me out into the courtyard. The feeling of oppression I'd experienced inside subsided a little but still lingered. There were too many windows, too many eyes, looking down on us from the building.

"Sit down," he said, gesturing to a tree stump. I obediently sat, my shaky legs abruptly giving way. I may be a loud mouth but I'm nowhere near as brave as I'd like you to think I am.

"Who the hell are you really?" I asked, looking up at him. He looked less, I don't know, *fluffy* than he had in the gondola, more together, more in charge. *More manly* I gibbered to myself. Really? Was I really starting all that nonsense after the shock I'd just had?

Will smiled. "I could tell you, but then I'd have to kill you." He must've noticed that my face was still white, because he quickly added, "No not really. You're safe with me."

He perched on the edge of the tree stump next to me. "I'm with Interpol –" he started.

I looked at him in surprise. "But you said you were a consultant – I thought you were in IT or something!"

"Well, I am a consultant. I never said it was IT. I'm working with the local police on something. That's why we're here – my colleagues are checking out reports of suspicious behaviour on the island."

"Unsavoury locals..." I murmured. He looked surprised. "You said the other day – they suspect unsavoury locals of –"

"Doing unsavoury things, yes." He grinned at me. "I would've warned you off properly but I thought it would make you even more determined to come here if I did. You're not the first writer I've met, you know."

"So what do you think has been happening here, then?"

"We think the local crime gangs use this place to stash things or for dead letter drops," he said.

I was intrigued. "What, you mean like drugs, or ill gotten gains or something?"

"Yes. And occasionally dead bodies."

"Oh. Right."

"So if I'd been up front and told you that, would that have stopped you coming here?"

I laughed. "Shit, no! I'd have got here even quicker."

He laughed at that too. "See, I was right. Writers!"

We sat for a moment, enjoying the peace and the sunshine, then Will stood up.

"Right," he said decisively. "I'd better tell my colleagues they can stop searching because it was my mad English writer friend the fishermen spotted last night –"

"Hold it right there!" I interrupted. "I wasn't here last night."

He turned back towards me. "You didn't camp here over night? That wasn't you, waving a torch around at midnight?"

I shook my head. *Ooh this is getting exciting* I thought. *Bugger! Left my notebook on the boat.*

Will looked around, then pulled me to my feet. "Come on, we need to get you off the island," he said, looking serious. "Where's Gino moored?"

"By the bridge," I said.

He kept hold of my hand and led me across the courtyard, through another building and out into another clearing. I looked around; we were in the yard at the foot of the old bell tower.

"We're going the wrong way," I pointed out.

"Damn, I don't know this island very well," said Will.

We stopped in the centre of the yard and looked around trying to get our bearings. I felt those icy prickles slowly trace their way across my skin again, goosebumps rising – I really didn't like being here. I thought of the ghost of old Doctor Paolo and shivered, wishing my imagination could be this active when I was sitting in front of my laptop faced with a blank page.

"Let's get out of here –" I started, tripping on something as I turned to Will. He caught me (which I didn't mind at all.)

"Are you okay?" he asked anxiously, peering into my face.

"I'm fine, I just trod on something. Probably the bones of a plague victim or one of Doctor Paolo's poor patients..."

I bent down and picked it up. A wallet. Will held his hand out.

"Let me see?" He opened it and flicked through the contents for some ID.

I craned my neck to see, curiosity getting the better (for the moment) of my nervousness. "Dr Santino Gerbasi," I read from an identity card. "Is he one of your Mafia people?"

"No. And you shouldn't go round calling them the Mafia. It can get you into all sorts of trouble." Will spoke matter of factly, his attention on the wallet rather than me. "You have to be –"

There was a dull thud behind me. Will stopped, mid-sentence, face frozen in shock. I wanted to turn around but, at the same time, turning around was the very last thing I thought I should do. One glance at Will's horrified expression, eyes fixed on the ground behind me, confirmed my suspicion.

"What –" I began to turn but Will's hand whipped out and grabbed me.

"Don't turn round!" he said, swallowing hard.

"The bell tower's behind me, isn't it?" I said, carefully. "Did something – did someone just jump off the bell tower?"

"Nooo," said Will slowly. I relaxed. "He definitely didn't jump..."

I shook off Will's hand and turned around. And instantly wished I hadn't.

On the ground in front of us sprawled the figure of a man. His head lolled at a weird angle; I couldn't work out why, until I saw that it was half-severed from the rest of his body by the thick chain around his neck.

The human body was not meant to hit the ground (or anything, really) with such force, particularly not a frail, elderly male body. I wanted to tear my eyes away but I couldn't. I could hear Will's worried voice coming to me, suddenly very far away, and then my body took over and made the decision to close my eyes for me.

I fainted.

CHAPTER NINE

I was only vaguely aware of everything that happened next. Will caught me (staggering slightly under my weight – I wasn't out of it enough to miss that) and laid me down gently on the ground, calling for help.

Two uniformed *polizia* ran out of the bushes and into the courtyard, stopping dead at the sight of the body on the floor (the other body on the floor, not me). One of them turned around and noisily threw up as Will bent over me, talking softly, his warm fingers gently stroking the hair away from my face.

I came round enough to stand up, wobbling shakily, and allowed him to lead me back through the woods, all the way to the bridge where Gino stood waiting for me accompanied by a grim-faced man in a suit. Gino nodded to Will in recognition as the other man turned to me angrily.

"So, this is the *signora* who has had half the police in Venice searching the island!" he started.

Will put up his hand to stop him. "Inspector Manera, Miss –

Jones - had nothing to do with it. There's a body in the bell tower yard," he said.

Gino's mouth dropped open; the Inspector looked from me to Will and back again. "A body? Do we know who?" he asked.

Will handed him the wallet. "We found this just before the body – er –"

"Dropped out of the bell tower and nearly hit us," I supplied. Will nodded.

"Yes. I didn't get a very close look at the victim but I think this is him."

Inspector Manera pulled out a credit card and studied it, almost dropping it.

"Santino Gerbasi. Do you know him?" I asked.

Manera calmly put the card back in the wallet. "No, I do not know the name."

"But the face rings a bell," I said. Will looked at me, quizzically. The hysteria was starting to well up again. "Can I sit down?" I said. "I feel a bit weird."

Will helped me sit down on the stone steps, and I sat taking deep breaths while the three men talked over my head, babbling away to each other in Italian. Even without knowing the language, it was clear that the Inspector was furious with Gino for bringing me over to the island, while Gino was on the defensive and Will played the peace maker. It was starting to get heated until Will spoke firmly, mentioning my name. I looked up at them, feeling like a ridiculous helpless female as they all stared back at me.

Will smiled gently and sat next to me, taking my hand. "Ok, Gino's going to take you home – all the way home, yes Gino?"

Gino nodded. "Right to your door, signora."

I smiled gratefully. "Thank you. You don't need to –"

"Yes he does," said Will, firmly. "You go home, clean up, relax, and I'll come round later to take your statement. Is that ok?"

I nodded. "Yes, thank you. I'm fine, honestly." I stood up, my legs no longer quite as shaky. "See? Fully recovered."

Inspector Manera barked one last admonishment at Gino as he pushed past him, glaring, and headed towards the bell tower. Gino shrugged and made a rude gesture, pulling a face at the Inspector's back as he climbed down the stairs and started untying the boat.

Will reached out to help me into the boat but I hesitated. "What's the matter?" he asked.

"Well if you're coming to see me later you'll need my address, won't you?" I said. "I mean, I know you're with Interpol and you could probably find me, but it'd be easier if I just gave it to you..."

Will laughed. "Of course, yes. Silly me. Here –" He took a small notebook – a proper policeman's notebook – from his pocket and passed it to me with a pen. I wrote down Francesca's address and he put it away without looking. I got into the boat and sat down.

As Gino went to jump into the boat Will grabbed his arm and spoke seriously to him; Gino nodded. Will watched grimly as Gino pushed the boat away from the steps and into the canal, starting the engine.

"What was all that about?" I asked. Gino smiled, charmingly and, I thought, falsely.

"He made me promise to take good care of you," he said.

I looked back and waved as we chugged out of the channel and into the open sea, leaving Will, the police and the almost-headless body of Dr Gerbasi far behind us.

64

Gino didn't get the chance to fulfil his promise to Will. The trip back to his boat shed gave me plenty of time to recover and, by the time we moored at Fondamente Zattere, I felt fine. The minute Gino leapt out of the boat and began tying it off, his old Papa waddled out from the boat shed, babbling furiously. Gino held up his hands in defence, trying to placate the angry geriatric, giving me the perfect opportunity to slip away and wander home. I wanted to be left alone with my thoughts for a while.

I was feeling a little bit ashamed of myself for fainting. The unfortunate doctor's body wasn't the first one I'd seen, although to be fair it was the first one that had hurled itself at me from a great height and just missed. It was also the only one that had almost been decapitated; I'd never seen the inside of someone's throat before and I wasn't hugely keen to repeat the experience.

After my first DCI Fletcher book hit the bestseller lists, I realised that I had to try and be more accurate in some of my procedural and technical terms (it was actually my third book and up to that point I'd kind of winged it and made stuff up). Luckily enough, one of my fans was also a forensic medical examiner, and she invited me along to a post mortem.

I'd stared at the body on the stainless steel table, naked, bruised (and dead, obviously) but otherwise cleaned up, cold and sterile, and tried to connect the sad lump of lifeless flesh with the person who'd inhabited it; the person who'd maybe had a job they hated, who'd had lots of friends or cats or was a hermit or loved chocolate as much as I did – who'd had the same kind of life we all have – but I couldn't. It was just a vessel. I didn't feel horror, or nausea, or disgust, just this huge, empty nothing.

And then my new friend (the medical examiner, not the corpse) started her examination. I lasted until the whirr of the bone saw started up (about 30 seconds) and then all I remember was the feel of cold lino against my cheek and wondering, *what the fuck am I doing on the floor?* And then I puked on her shoes.

Surprisingly enough, she was still my friend after that but, less surprisingly, I never went to a post mortem examination again; I just used to go along afterwards and see what she'd discovered. Internal organs, once removed and put in a jar, far, far away from the host's body, are just another lump of meat after all.

I crossed the Grand Canal on a *gondola traghetto*, a kind of gondola ferry, and got back to Francesca's apartment in no time at all. As I unlocked the front door I could hear the old girl upstairs again, not arguing this time, but sobbing. Really sobbing, as if her heart was not just broken but smashed into smithereens; obliterated by grief. I hesitated; should I knock on her door and check on her? She sounded in a bad way, but what could I do when we didn't speak the same language?

Sod it, I could still show her that I was there if she needed help. I stepped back and looked up; her window was open. I knocked on her door; no answer, but maybe she hadn't heard me? I knocked again, loudly, and this time the sobbing stopped abruptly.

I waited but she didn't come down. I stepped back again as I heard a noise from above, and noticed that the window was now shut. So she didn't want help; fair enough. I lifted the flap on the letterbox a little way and called out to her.

"Buongiorno! Er – it's Bella, from downstairs. Are you ok? Just let me know if you need anything." I waited for a reply but none came. She was probably just waiting for the bloody nosey *inglese* woman to bugger off and leave her alone. I shrugged; I'd tried.

I went inside.

CHAPTER TEN

A cup of tea makes everything better. I sat at the desk in front of the window, steaming mug in hand, doors open onto the balcony, and felt more alive than I had done in ages. Which may make me a terrible person, but it's also what makes me a writer.

I flipped open the laptop, mind buzzing, but before I could start – the phone rang. Susie. I suddenly realised that I hadn't rung her for three days, despite promising to keep her informed and let her know that Francesca wasn't a crazy person who had skinned me alive and was now wearing me as a Bella suit.

I answered. "Ciao, *salsiccia piccola!*"

Susie sounded puzzled. "Hello little sausage?"

I glared at my laptop. "What? Shit, this translation website is crap..."

"So anyway –" Susie always knew when I was about to go off on a tangent and was adept at steering the conversation back into normal waters. "How's Venice?"

"Full of canals and over-emotional Italians. No, actually it's great."

"So, are you....?"

"Writing? I was just about to start when you rang. The perfect story almost fell into my lap today. Or on my head, to be more accurate."

"Ok...I have no idea what you're talking about, should that worry me?"

I shut my eyes for a moment and pictured the body at my feet, in the shadow of the bell tower. If I told Susie what had happened that morning, she'd either be over on the next flight (I love her but – no, not when I'm trying to write), or demanding my safe return to London. Neither scenario was that appealing.

"No," I said. "I'm just being enigmatic. I –"

"Oh my god, you've met someone, haven't you?" she burst out.

"What are you, a witch?" I laughed.

"Who is he, some Italian stallion? Is he tanned and gorgeous?"

"No, he's an albino midget with a wooden leg, no teeth and a bad toupee, but he HAS got a massive –"

"I get it, stop prying Susie!" She sounded exasperated but in a good way. "But you're ok, yeah? I was getting a bit worried when I hadn't heard from you."

I felt a sudden rush of love for my friend and almost wished that she was here with me, enjoying a few glasses of prosecco, taking in the sights and laughing at my terrible jokes (*Doge stop me now, I'm having such a good time...*).

"I'm fine," I said, feeling a bit teary. Maybe having a corpse flung at me was affecting me more than I realised... "But I'm going to hang up now and start writing before I lose the plot."

"You lost the plot years ago, darling."

"Ayeeee thank you..."

"Say hello to Guiseppe for me," she laughed.

"You are so far off the mark it's not true," I said, and disconnected the call.

I leaned back in my chair, put my fingers together and cracked them in a *'let's get down to business'* manner, then started typing.

UNTITLED VENETIAN MYSTERY by Annabelle Tyson(Working title: Hey Dude Where's My Gondola)
Chapter One (actually more like Chapter Three, can't think of the beginning, I'll come back to that)

Ella stood in the courtyard, looking up at the bell tower as it poked – thrust (ooh er) – its way into the blue sky like a crumbling stone beacon. The hot sun filtered through the trees, casting a shadow over her tanned face.

(Or night time? More atmos?)

A gentle night breeze caressed Ella's firm tanned arms as she waited in the dark. Out there, beyond the trees, beyond the ruins of the abandoned hospital, stars lit up the night sky, but in here the blackness was absolute; not just darkness, but the total absence of any light. It was if the crumbling bell tower that loomed over her oppressively had sucked the – something – out of the landscape. (Oh YES this is more like it). Essence? Lifeblood? Life force?

Ella didn't scare easily, but she shivered as something moved in the foliage overwhelming the decaying building behind her. She shone her torch around, its beam picking out two round, glowing eyes. The owl hooted in alarm and took flight. She shook her head at her own nervousness and waited.

"You came." His voice sent a thrill down her spine. She turned around and saw Bill – Tim – Tom – TOM! – She turned and there stood Tom, watching her.

It was a start, I supposed... Kidding myself that I still didn't know who my hero Tom was going to be, I sat back and composed the scene in my head.

He was short for a hero – about 5'6", 5'7". Nice eyes, big friendly smile, short brown hair thinning slightly and greying at the temples. Middle class – a bit posh, well certainly compared to me. Looked like an IT consultant but wasn't.

Tom took her hands (where did he take them?! Bring them back, you monster!!!!)

Tom held both her hands in his, his skin soft and warm but his touch firm (oooh yeah...) and gazed deeply into her eyes.

"You came," he said again. "You shouldn't have come. It's dangerous."

Ella tossed her silky blonde hair imperiously, hoping she looked more confident than she actually felt.

"I'm not scared," she claimed. "I don't need protecting!"

"No, but I bloody do!" said Tom.

And then he kissed her, softly, on the lips. Ella liked it and wanted more – much more. Ooh Ella, you minx!

She took him in her arms and puckered up, holding him, leaning in for a great big Hollywood style kiss that went on and on –

She was interrupted by an abrupt knocking at the door. Surprised, Ella let go of Tom, who hit the ground with a high-pitched squeal...

I shook my head to bring myself back to reality. It was getting dark, and someone actually was knocking at my door. I snapped the laptop shut and answered.

It was Will. I could feel my cheeks starting to burn.

"Oh! Hello!" I said. "Do you want to come in?"

"That depends," he smiled. "Have you eaten?"

———

We went to a small but busy restaurant on the Fondamenta San Lorenzo, where the waiter greeted Will like an old friend. He found us a table next to the canal and left us to study the menu.

"They know you," I said. "You often bring witnesses here for questioning?"

"Oh yes," smiled Will, sipping at his Aperol spritz (the Venetian aperitif of choice - I thought they looked like Iron Bru and tasted revolting). "This is standard practice over here, far more civilised than the way we do things back in England. Of course the level of wining and dining depends on the severity of crime you've witnessed. A three-course meal with wine and cheese to finish is quite typical for your average gruesome murder.

An armed robbery, now that would only qualify you for a trip to McDonalds, although I could probably justify you 'going large' if it was a particularly violent one."

"What about shoplifting? What would that entitle me to?"

"A Ginsters pasty from an all-night garage," he said promptly. We both laughed.

"No, I live a few streets away and I've been here a few times," he said. "I'm basically working my way through the entire menu..."

We ate and drank, carefully avoiding all talk of the day's earlier events.

"So you write crime novels?" he asked. "What's a nice girl like you doing writing about murders?"

I laughed. "What makes you think I'm nice?"

He smiled, a little shy again. My heart did a little flip and slowly began to melt around the edges. *Pull yourself together, woman!*

"Why do you think crime is so popular?" he asked, fiddling with his wine glass. I laughed.

"You're better placed to answer that than me," I said. He grinned.

"No, I mean as a genre. Crime novels. Some of the most popular authors are crime writers – Jo Nesbo, Lee Child, Iain Rankin – "

I waited for him to say 'Annabelle Tyson' and was stupidly affronted when he didn't, even though the last thing I wanted was for him to put two and two together and realise I'd lied to him. I still wasn't entirely sure why I had.

"And TV," he said. "Every other programme's a cop show."

I sat back and pursed my lips, as if I was giving it some thought, but I already knew what I was going to say. It was my go-to interview sound bite, and the reason (kind of) why I write what I do.

"I think it's because everyone has the potential to be a killer," I said. He looked slightly shocked. "Everyone has a trigger, something that would tip them over the edge."

"Like what?" He stared intently into my eyes. I shifted uncomfortably.

"Like – protecting family. Protecting someone you love who can't protect herself."

I cursed myself for over-elaborating. He stared at me silently for a moment, and then nodded. "Yes, I can see that. Protecting others."

We both reached for the wine bottle in the silence that followed and laughed. Will took it, pouring more wine for me first, then himself.

"I'm sorry I was such an idiot earlier, passing out like that –" I began, but he stopped me.

"You weren't an idiot! I nearly passed out too, and I've seen a lot of dead bodies," he said.

"I've seen a few too, in the morgue. But none of them looked like that..."

He reached out to touch my hand, then gently pulled away again.

"Bodies in the morgue can't prepare you for seeing something like that," he said softly.

We stared at the canal for a moment.

"I found a body on a beach once," I said. He looked at me. "That's what made me write my first novel. I wanted to solve the murder."

"I see." He waited while I gathered my thoughts. "What happened?"

I could still see it, clear as day. Clearer.

I never set out to be a novelist; people from the part of South London I grew up in don't do things like that. When you go to a school like Eton or Roedean, the question when you finish your exams is 'Oxford or Cambridge?' But at my school it was 'Tesco or Sainsburys?'

I was the first one in my family to go to university, which coincidentally also made me the first one to drop out. When I left halfway through a Theatre Studies degree I didn't really know what to do with myself, but I had this vague idea about being a travel writer, partly because the Rough Guide and Lonely Planet books were starting to become very popular, but mostly because it sounded like a brilliant excuse to have lots of holidays. And I really didn't want to move back home.

So I packed a rucksack and set off. I travelled around Central and South America, seeing Mayan temples, pyramids and waterfalls, meeting incredible people and getting into scrapes (I nearly got kidnapped by drug runners but ended up going to a rave in the jungle with them instead). It was a road trip of epic proportions.

The only problem was, I was so busy having fun (and trying not to get kidnapped) that I didn't write a single word.

My last stop before home was Rio. I hated it and loved it in equal measure – the city and its people were colourful and vibrant, but the poverty, the slums, the children running around eating garbage and being treated like vermin – that I wasn't so keen on.

On my last day I got up at dawn, unable to sleep for thoughts of the trip back to London and what was waiting for me at home in dull, dreary Croydon, and went for a walk along the beach.

Even at this early hour, the sun was hot and bright enough to bleach the colour from the landscape, but not from the sea; the deep, sparkling blue contrasted with sand that was so fine, so golden, it was almost white. Even with my sunglasses on I had to squint a little from the glare.

And that was where I found him.

He was little, and achingly beautiful. Angelic. Olive skinned, big hazel eyes that gazed unseeingly at some point in the distance. Green shorts, ripped and dirty but still bright against the bleached sand. No t-shirt to hide the ugly bruises on his chest.

"A street kid?" asked Will, leaning forward in concern. I nodded grimly.

"That's what they said. 'Just' a street kid, no one important..." I saw it all again in my mind, as fresh as if it had happened yesterday. "I called the police and stayed with his body until they came, but I never found out what happened. I flew home that night."

Will poured me another glass of wine and I smiled at him gratefully.

"Thanks. I never forgot that little boy, because it – it didn't make sense to me. They said he was a street kid and these things happen – which is hardly an excuse - but he didn't look like a street kid to me. He looked loved, well fed. His clothes looked like they were expensive and although they were ripped and dirty, it just didn't look right. It looked like someone had taken a pair of scissors to them and rolled him about in the mud to make him *look* like a street kid." I smiled ruefully at Will. "Listen to me, trying to play detective!"

"No, your instincts were telling you it wasn't as simple as they were making it out to be," he said earnestly. "You have to trust your instincts. That's what a lot of detective work comes down to. Your instinct tells you something, and then you find the evidence to back it up. Or not, as the case may be."

We watched a gondola float along the canal next to us, the gondolier singing softly as an elderly couple sat in the back holding hands and gazing at each other adoringly. I smiled and turned to find Will watching me.

"What are your instincts telling you now?" I asked. He smiled.

We finished eating and strolled slowly back through the streets towards Francesca's apartment. Will clearly knew the city well; we wandered along the smaller side streets, across deserted piazzas, easily navigating the winding maze of Venetian canal paths even in the dark. He seemed very much at home.

"You picked the right city to write a supernatural mystery in," he said, as we turned another corner. "This place has so many legends and ghost stories attached to it. I've been to other parts of

Italy – Naples, and Rome – and they're beautiful, but none of them have the same atmosphere as Venice."

"It's because it's an island," I said, spotting another dead end, culminating in a dark canal, ahead of us. Will took my elbow and steered me through a narrow archway that led us into yet another passageway. I was completely lost by now. "Islands always have their own mythology, don't they? It's to do with being outsiders."

"Do you think that's what it is?" asked Will, interested. "Being an outsider?"

"I think so. Legends aren't just there to explain away who makes the lightning or stuff like that;they're there to connect people. As soon as you share a story with someone, you become part of the same tribe – you have these common references, or shared experiences. Maybe islanders feel like outsiders because they're not connected with the main land, either by their stories or geographically." Will was watching me, thoughtfully. I laughed. "Of course, I could be talking a load of absolute bollocks…"

"No, no, I get exactly what you mean. Venice is so close to the mainland, but for a large part of its history it wasn't part of Italy. It was on its own."

We turned into a small square.

"Also, don't forget that before the tourists started coming, a lot of Venetians were sailors or fishermen, and they've always been ones for superstitions and tales of the one that got away," I said.

"That's one thing Interpol agents have in common with them, then," said Will. "We've always got a story about the one that got away."

"Have you?" I asked, curiously. "Is there a crime you didn't solve, or a criminal you couldn't catch?"

Will looked at me for a moment, then walked over to an

ancient covered well in the centre of the square. Classic changing-the-subject behaviour. I made a note to ask him about the-one-that-got-away again when we were (*lovers!*) better acquainted...

"Do you know the story about the lady in white?" he said.

I laughed. "I think every culture has a story about a lady in white, haven't they?"

Will smiled. 'You might be right. But this one isn't your archetypal Grey Lady or ghost."

I joined him at the well and ran my hands over its smooth grey stone as Will began the story.

"Most of the squares in Venice had wells, like this one, for the residents to take their water from, although most of them have been filled in now. Sometimes in really hot weather the wells would start to run dry, and the city rulers had to ration supplies by limiting the times of day people could collect water – only in the morning, for example. Neighbours began to fight over the water, accusing others of taking more than their share, and in a lot of neighbourhoods the men would take it in turns to watch the well, to stop people stealing water after dark. One night, in this very square as a boatman stood guard, an elderly lady came to the well. She was clearly very poor, and she told the boatman that she had not had anything to eat or drink all day. She begged him to spare her a little water from the well to quench her thirst. But the boatman swore at her; he suspected that she was none other than his neighbour, playing a trick on him to get extra water. The boatman threatened her with the knife he used to cut fish from his nets during the day, saying that he would gut her just like a fish from the lagoon if she didn't leave."

A cool breeze ruffled Will's hair, blowing in from the nearby canal. It was still warm, but I shivered, my overactive imagination cranking up again.

"But the old lady just looked at him and repeated her request for water. This incensed the boatman, who still suspected a trick, and he stabbed the old lady, pulling away the veil that covered her head, expecting to see his neighbour. But she was just an old woman."

"Bah bah Bah!!!," I cried dramatically, completely ruining the mood. Will laughed.

"Quite. The boatman was horrified when he realised what he'd done, but instead of praying to God for forgiveness he stuffed the old lady's body into the well –"

"- Contaminating the water and killing the entire community –"

Will laughed again, this time with a hint of exasperation. "I know you're the storyteller, but are you going to let me finish this one?"

I hung my head in remorse. "Sorry, officer. You can arrest me if you like."

"Don't tempt me... Anyway, just as day broke the boatman fell into a terrible fever –"

"Probably from drinking contaminated water from the well –" I started. Will rolled his eyes. I said, "Sorry, couldn't help myself."

"His wife tried to calm his fever with cold water from the well, but he refused to drink it, saying it made him even thirstier. His throat burned and his temperature grew ever hotter, until finally he confessed his terrible crime. The old lady's body was pulled from the well, but as her corpse lay there it changed from that of a withered –

"Dead –"

"Yes, dead – old lady, into a beautiful lady dressed in white, an angel. The lady opened her eyes and said to the boatman, 'You may have refused to help a person in distress, but my Father never does'. And with that she dipped her hand into the well, which immediately began to overflow with cool clean water. She splashed a few drops onto the boatman's fevered brow and he was healed. And the well never ran dry again."

Will gave a little bow as I applauded him.

"Good story?" he asked.

"Yes. Tough crowd, though." I followed him out of the square. "Sorry about that. I always make stupid jokes or say something inappropriate when I'm feeling uncomfortable."

He stopped, turning to me seriously.

"You don't feel uncomfortable with me, do you? I assure you –"

"No, not at all!" I said quickly. "It was just your story – in that place."

"I wasn't trying to scare you," he said, clearly worried he'd upset me.

"Well, you did scare me a bit, but it was awesome!" I cried. He laughed, relieved.

I took his arm and we walked on.

Five minutes later we were outside Francesca's apartment.

"Well, thank you for a lovely evening," I said. *Invite him in! No, don't! Yes, do it!*

I ignored my inner monologue and leaned in to kiss him on the cheek. His face was warm and smooth and he smelt nice.

"I'm glad you enjoyed it," he said. *What – the kiss? Oh, the meal. Yes.* "I was wondering..."

YES! Whatever it is, yes, definitely.

"I was thinking, how would you like to work with me?" he asked, tentatively.

"Work with you?" I was surprised.

"On this murder. I just thought it might be a good starting point for your new book – unless you've already got an idea, of course."

"No, I haven't," I admitted, "I've got my two protagonists but nothing else." I blushed as I thought of the thinly-disguised Ella and Tom. "That would be great, but am I allowed to? Won't you get into trouble?"

"No," said Will. "Interpol often bring consultants into difficult or unusual cases, and this one's certainly unusual. Your creative instincts would bring something different to the investigation. I've just got a boring old policeman's brain, but you - you see things differently to me."

"Well – if you're sure you won't get into trouble –" I forced myself not to hop around with excitement.

"Is that a yes, then?" asked Will.

"Yes! Yes please." I tried hard to look like working with Interpol was just another day at the office for someone like me, but failed. He grinned.

"That's settled then."

We stood and smiled at each other. I wondered whether he'd try to kiss me, and he had just started to move in a little closer when a noise from above made us both jump, guiltily. I looked up; there was a light on in the elderly neighbour's window, illuminating the curtains as they twitched.

I laughed and gestured upwards. "I think we're being spied on," I said. Will looked up, then stepped away from me.

"Well, I'd better go. It's been a long day. I'll call you tomorrow." And with that he turned and fled.

I watched him go, then turned to that upstairs window. "Thanks a lot, you old passion killer," I said, and went inside.

CHAPTER ELEVEN

I climbed into bed that night with my mind spinning after the day's events and too many glasses of wine. I was convinced I'd never be able to sleep, but five minutes after my head hit the pillow I was in the Land of Nod.

I dreamed of Poveglia.

I sat on a rusting bed frame in the courtyard beneath the bell tower, enjoying the sunshine. Next to me, the corpse of the unfortunate Dr Gerbasi sat, head lolling at an uncomfortable angle.

I drank some water from a plastic bottle and passed it to my companion, trying not to notice the way the water leaked out from the massive gaping wound in his neck; I felt that it would be impolite to point it out. The water trickled over the thick rusty chain that had embedded itself in his skin.

"So..." I said, groping for something to say. "Nice day."

"Not really," the late Dr Gerbasi gurgled, damply. "Not for me, anyway."

"No, I suppose not." I thought it was terribly bad form for him to point out that he was dead when I'd just been trying to make polite conversation, but maybe the deceased don't go in for small talk.

"Not for him, either," said the corpse, pointing up at the bell tower. Something twisted and turned high up, struggling against the bonds that held it in the air. I narrowed my eyes to see more clearly.

It was Will, gasping for air as he clawed at the rusty chain around his neck, face starting to turn blue.

I opened my mouth to scream –

The piercing shriek woke me from my nightmare, but it wasn't me screaming.

I sat bolt upright in bed, heart pounding, head swimming. It took me a couple of seconds to realise that the scream had come from upstairs.

I flung on my dressing gown and raced into the living room, stopping to listen for more cries of distress. From above I could hear the elderly neighbour crying and moaning in a low voice; her words weren't very clear, but it sounded like *'no, no, mio Dio no!'*

I ran out of the house and banged on her door. I could still hear her crying and talking earnestly, pleading with someone. Holy fuck, was someone attacking her? Her door was firmly shut though, with no signs of a break in.

And then I heard another voice, so deep and low I *felt* it, reverberating in my chest, rather than heard it.

"Ci vediamo all'inferno, puttana!"

I shuddered in horror: *what the fuck was that?* I banged on the door furiously, harder than ever, shouting out. *"Signora*, are you ok? Shall I call the police?"

And then the door was flung open.

"Holy shit!" I yelped. Were all my conversations with her destined to start that way?

She stood in front of me, eerily still. Her hair was tucked into a ridiculous, old-fashioned nightcap and her pale skin glowed in the moonlight, almost white. *Alabaster.* Ghost-like. She looked me up and down, her clenched fingers the only sign of tension.

"Incubo," she said, calmly. I frowned.

"I'm sorry, I don't –"

"Incubo. A – a dream - bad –" she said.

"A bad dream? A nightmare?" I thought it must've been a terrible nightmare to elicit that scream. "Is there someone else there? I heard a voice."

"Voice?" She looked puzzled; she didn't understand the word.

"A voice. A man. A *signore.* Er – an *uomo?*" I struggled to remember the rudimentary bits of the lingo I'd picked up. She shook her head.

"No! *No uomo.* No man! Bad dream!" She went to shut the door but I stuck out my hand to stop her.

"Are you ok?"

She looked at me, nakedly, and for a moment her eyes swam with tears. But then the shutters came down. She glared at me and shook her head, slamming the door shut and almost trapping my fingers.

I went back to bed, still shaken, but this time there was no getting back to sleep. I gave up, made a cup of hot chocolate and, propping myself up on the pillows, lay back with Francesca's book in hand.

I looked up the story of the mad doctor on Poveglia and re-read it.

After years of torturing his poor patients in the name of medical science, the demented physician had become convinced that the island was haunted; first with the spirits of those long-dead plague sufferers, but then, as his conscience finally began to prick him, with the vengeful ghosts of his victims.

Finally he could bear it no more. One sunny morning the evil doctor had climbed the bell tower, tormented and driven insane by the voices of his former patients, and thrown himself off, landing in the courtyard below – right where I'd been standing earlier, by the sound of it.

However, unlike the unfortunate Dr Gerbasi, he'd survived the fall. Not for long. From nowhere – on this bright, beautiful summer's day – a strange mist had seeped into the courtyard and now hovered over the doctor's broken and helpless body. The horrified medical staff who, at the sound of his screams, had run to help, arrived just in time to see their boss slowly enveloped in the suffocating cloud, a cloud that no longer looked like mist, but had the suggestion of arms and legs reaching out to violently pummel the doctor's body, tossing it around like a lifeless ragdoll. The doctor let out one last agonising howl of pain and suddenly the mist was gone, along with the life from his battered and bruised corpse.

His victims had extracted their revenge...

Was it just a coincidence that our victim today had also been a doctor? The story was widely known in the city, and someone had gone to great lengths to carry him up the bell tower, stringing him up with that thick chain which in itself must weigh a ton. They were obviously making a point. So did that mean his murderer was a victim of something he'd done in the past? Or murderers – that was a lot of work for someone on their own; taking the body over to the island (or had he been persuaded to meet them there? He might have been killed on Poveglia), then chaining him up.

Or was it suicide? It was a hell of a lot of work to kill yourself, but maybe if he were guilty of some kind of malpractice and his conscience had kicked in, killing himself in that place might have been a way of admitting his guilt and making amends.

So many questions... But there was no way of working it out tonight – I looked at the clock – or rather, this morning. I yawned; the hot chocolate was working, despite the thoughts whirling in my brain. I reached over, clicked off the light and was asleep within minutes.

CHAPTER TWELVE

The next day was as sunny as the last one. I opened the shutters and breathed in the scent of the sea. *I could get used to this* I thought.

As I dressed, I listened out for any sounds from the apartment above, but there was nothing. Maybe it had just been a bad dream. I tried to forget that deep gravelly voice I'd heard; maybe I'd imagined it. But I knew I hadn't.

Will had promised to call me, but I had no idea when. I flipped open the laptop and started to write. By which I mean that I read back what I'd written the day before and deleted half of it. Things were definitely looking up, though; last week, I'd have deleted the whole thing and thrown the laptop into the canal. Maybe my writer's block was becoming a thing of the past.

The morning came and went. I couldn't concentrate; I'd write a few lines, then delete them, then write a bit more, save that, get up, stand on the balcony, make a cup of tea, forget about it, throw out the cold cup of tea, eat a biscuit – I'd driven myself in-fucking-sane by 11.30.

When the phone finally rang I literally pounced on it like a hungry tiger pouncing on an antelope (or whatever it is hungry tigers eat).

"*Buongiorno!*" I said, far more calmly than I felt. "You have reached the Sunshine Home for Terminally Bewildered Crime Writers, please come and rescue me after the beep..."

Will laughed. "The new book's going well today, then is it?" he asked.

"It's okkayyy...." I said.

"I'd better not disturb you then –"

"No! God, no, please disturb me! I really need disturbing!"

"Oh I don't know, you sound pretty disturbed already." Will laughed again.

"Oh ha ha..." *He's got a nice laugh.* "What's happening? Have you got anywhere with the investigation?"

"Join me for a coffee and I can tell you what I've found out so far..."

"Ok." I shut the laptop down and reached for my bag. "Where are you?"

There was a knock on the front door.

"Outside."

We strolled to Piazza San Marco and found a table outside Caffe

Florian. After ordering two monstrously expensive café lattes Will took a file from the leather messenger bag he was carrying.

"What's this?" I asked, curiously.

"Background on the victim," he said, taking out some photos. I glanced at the top one and looked away again quickly; it showed the corpse, neck wound and bloody chain in close up. Will noticed and shoved it under the pile of papers. "Sorry."

"I was thinking about where he was killed, and how." I stopped and smiled at the waiter bringing our coffee, waiting for him to leave before continuing. "I was thinking, it can't be a coincidence that he was a doctor, being killed in that manner, in that place. Maybe there was some malpractice –"

Will shook his head. "He wasn't that sort of doctor. He was a PhD, not a medical doctor."

"Oh." I felt vaguely disappointed, my theory destroyed at the first hurdle. "No victims seeking revenge, then."

Will fingered the pile of papers and photographs uneasily. "What is it?" I asked, concerned.

"Well... he wasn't a physician, he was a teacher. Retired. He taught Classics and Latin in some very exclusive private schools, all over Europe." Will took out a sheet of paper. There was a long list of what I assumed were schools, in France, Italy, even a couple in the UK. "There's nothing on his record, but he did appear to leave a couple of those schools quite abruptly."

"What do you mean?"

"Most teachers would give their eye teeth for a position at any one of those schools. Especially one teaching Latin."

"I didn't know they even taught Latin anymore," I said. Will smiled.

"State schools don't, but most public schools do. The sort of schools where all the students are being groomed for a future career in Law or Medicine."

"Posh schools."

"Ha, yes, 'posh' schools." Will grinned. "I must be posh then."

"You are!" I said.

"So, anyway, this means if you've got a job at one of these 'posh' schools, you'll probably do all you can to hang on to it. Not leave half way through term. That's terribly bad form."

I giggled.

"Sorry, was that too posh for you?" Will asked with a smile.

"Oh DAHLING, you're altogether far too posh for the likes of me! But joking aside – if he left a job –"

"Two jobs, actually."

"If he left two jobs at really good schools in the middle of term, which was bound to piss off the people in charge and hamper the chances of him scoring a job in another good school –"

"There had to be a pretty compelling reason for him to leave. Yes. It doesn't say on his record, but I think he probably *had* to leave. Either because he was given the choice between resigning or being sacked, or..."

"Or because he knew he was about to get caught." I finished. "Get caught doing what?"

Will raised an eyebrow. "What do you think?"

I stared at him in astonishment. "Not – not interfering with the children? But surely if that had been the case he wouldn't have been able to carry on teaching –"

Will laughed bitterly.

"Ah, but if it had come out that one of the masters was fiddling with the boys, think of the scandal! Think of the parents, rushing to take their children out of the school! All those lost fees... No school wants buggery on their glossy Prospectus."

I was horrified.

"But – they couldn't have covered it up! Even if they'd let him go without making a fuss, surely they would've made it impossible for him to get another job? They couldn't have given him a reference –"

"You'd be surprised. Remember, if he was applying for jobs at other public schools, those schools would've been rivals. If it got out that, I don't know, Eton for example, had been employing a paedophile, there are plenty of schools that would be eager to capitalise on that."

"So they were happy to let a paedophile carry on teaching, and probably molesting, other kids, as long as their fucking reputation went untarnished? For god's sake!" I shook my head angrily. "Give me a crappy comprehensive school any day, in that case."

Will didn't speak, just sipped at his coffee. I watched a small child running around the piazza, scattering pigeons and giggling while her parents argued over where to eat lunch. I felt sick.

"It sounds like he got what he fucking deserved," I said.

We walked slowly back to Francesca's apartment. I still felt sick to my stomach to think of the dead teacher being given free rein to carry on with his perverted deeds, but it did make me feel a whole lot less sorry about the gruesome end he'd come to.

We reached the front door, Will turning to me and taking my hands in his.

93

"Are you ok?" he asked, concerned. "I can see how much this has shocked you."

"I'm fine," I said. "The thought of him being allowed to just carry on - "

"Remember, this is just conjecture," Will said. "We don't know that any of this actually happened."

"I bet it bloody did, though!" I said hotly.

"His past does look suspicious," he admitted.

"Can I have the list of schools?" I asked. "I'd like to do some digging."

Will nodded and took the piece of paper from the file.

"I haven't given you this, of course," he said.

"Of course." I took it from him. "Well I –"

Before I could finish speaking, Will leant in and kissed me.

Have you ever really, really wanted to kiss someone, and then finally it happens and it's a complete let down?

It wasn't that kind of kiss.

Have you ever really, really wanted to kiss someone, someone you're really into even though you don't know them very well and it's been a long time since you kissed anyone and you're not even sure if you remember how to do it –

And then suddenly, everything disappears and all that's left is the two of you. All your thoughts, your feelings, all your nerve endings, everything is concentrated on your mouth and his mouth, on the softness of his lips and his gently probing tongue, the warmth of his breath on your face, the smoothness of his cheek, the way his nose fits against yours...you're completely, utterly, totally lost in that moment, lost in each other. After a while other parts of your body wake up and start to join in the fun (yes nipples, I'm talking about you!) and parts of his body too (well hello there!), but all there is in that blissful moment is the kiss, pure and simple.

That's the kind of kiss it was. And then some.

We parted – eventually – both a little out of breath.

"Sorry, I couldn't help –" Will began. I stopped him with another kiss, just a peck this time, and smiled at him.

"You really don't have to apologise for that!" I said.

He grinned. "Oh good!"

We smiled at each other, neither wanting the moment to end, but it had to. From the upstairs apartment I could hear the elderly neighbour stomping about. I opened my mouth to tell Will about the events of last night, with the screaming and the spooky voice, but he spoke first.

"Oh god, is that the time? I'm so sorry, Bella, I really have to go," he said, looking at his watch.

"Oh." I was disappointed. "I thought maybe you might want to come in –"

"Some of us are meant to be working!" He smiled ruefully. "I'm supposed to be filling Inspector Manera in on our victim's background. Don't tell him, but I told you first..."

I laughed. "You really know how to spoil a lady!"

An upstairs window opened noisily, making Will jump.

"I have to go, but I'll call you later," he said.

"Promise?"

"I promise."

A quick kiss on the lips, a last lingering look, and he was off. I watched him go, sighing wistfully, then scolded myself for behaving like a character in a cut-price Mills and Boon and went inside.

CHAPTER THIRTEEN

I sat down to write and on cue, the phone rang.

"Susie!" I cried. "How the devil are you?"

"You sound very chipper," she said, suspiciously. "No dodgy Italian today?"

"There are plenty of dodgy Italians but I've given up trying to speak it," I told her.

"How's the Italian Stallion?" she asked, eager for gossip. I thought of Will – mild mannered, middle class, terribly English Will – and laughed.

"He's not Italian –"

"Ah ha!" she cried triumphantly. "So there is someone! Come on, spill!"

Damn it! "Don't you want to ask me how the book's going?"

"Screw the book, tell me about your love life."

I sighed. There was no getting out of it. "Ok. He's sweet and a little bit shy and funny –"

"English?"

"Very English - a bit posh, actually. Even posher than you. In his 40s, dark hair…"

"Good in bed?"

"I don't bloody know! I've only been here a week, give me a chance."

"All right, good kisser then?"

Another sigh – this time a dreamy, wistful, Jane Austen heroine type of sigh – escaped me. Susie pounced.

"Oh my god, he is!"

"How old are you, twelve? Ask me about the book, please."

I managed to steer the conversation onto the more serious matter of my writing and how it was essential (for the book, obviously…) that I stayed in Venice for the foreseeable future. As we talked my eyes strayed onto the sheet of paper Will had given me, and a light bulb suddenly flicked on as I recognised one of the schools on the list.

"Right," I said, finally. "Inspiration has just struck me and I have to write something down right now before I forget it."

"Ok," said Susie, a little put out by my abrupt manner. "Well, say hello to –"

"I will. Bye!" I disconnected the call and felt bad for a moment. But it passed. It always does.

I hadn't spotted it earlier – too horrified by the rest of the conversation to read the list properly – but I was sure I knew someone at one of the schools.

I'd been part of a crime writers' mentoring scheme a few years ago, and one of my protégés (who'd been an excellent writer but should, I felt, have tried another genre as he was altogether too nice to write really nasty murders) had been an English teacher at a private school. He was only in his 30s, so wouldn't have been there when the late doctor was teaching, but he might be able to find out a little more about what had happened there and (more importantly) who to.

IF he was still teaching there himself. It was a long shot but I thought it was worth a try.

I searched through my email contacts and found him: Charlie McArthur. He had a much better writer's name then me, I'd always thought. We'd kept in contact for a while after the mentoring scheme ended, but it had been a while now since I'd last heard from him.

I emailed him, then went into the bedroom to get a light cardigan – it suddenly felt a bit chilly.

Francesca's book lay open, face down, on the bed. I glanced at it as I went to the wardrobe, then stopped.

I hadn't left it on the bed.

I'm very particular about my bed. I always make it the minute I get up so it's ready when I go back to sleep at night. I might lay the odd item of clothing on it as I dress, but then I straighten it out again so it's just so. The rest of my house can (and often does) descend into chaos, but my bedroom is always an oasis of peace and calm and tidiness.

I DID NOT LEAVE THAT BOOK THERE.

I also never leave books open like that. I love books and I treat them with respect. People who turn over the corners of pages or leave books open, flattening out or even -- *shudder* -- breaking their spines should be shot. I would never have left that book, like that, there.

I reached out and plucked it off the bed, turning it over as I began to close it. And then I stopped.

It was open at the beginning of a story. I'd read all of them at least once so far, the ones that had really struck me two or three times, but I didn't remember this one. I sat down on the bed and started to read.

I woke up a couple of hours later, the book lying next to me where it had dropped out of my sleepy fingers. The events of the past couple of days (and nights) had caught up with me.

I stretched, feeling much better after what in my youth we used to call a 'disco nap' (a sleep during the day to build up my energy for a long night of partying ahead) but nowadays was much more accurately named a 'nana nap'. I must be getting old.

Tummy rumbling, I headed into the kitchen just as my phone beeped with a text message. Will.

Sorry am tied up with something at work. Looks like an all-nighter. Promise I will call you tomorrow. W x

Disappointed, but hoping he'd managed to grab a disco nap himself, I put the kettle on, stretched again and resolved to go to the supermarket. All these dinners in fancy restaurants were taking the toll on my waistline.

I came back from the shop, laden with bread, cheese, cold meats and all sorts of lovely food (but no chocolate biscuits). I put the shopping down on the doorstep as I hunted through my bag for the key.

In the upstairs apartment, I could hear the elderly neighbour talking urgently to someone again. I stopped searching so I could listen properly (what can I say? I'm a writer and therefore entitled to eavesdrop as part of my research into human behaviour).

I half hoped, half feared hearing that horrible male voice again. But from what I could hear, this conversation was completely one-sided. She was on the phone, talking insistently, not arguing exactly but definitely having what my parents used to call a 'heated debate'. I wished again that I could understand the language.

The talking stopped and I waited for a moment, but no more came. I fumbled around again for my key and then jumped out of my skin as the door next to me suddenly opened.

She looked as surprised as I felt, for a change. Still wearing the ridiculous floppy hat, she nodded curtly to me as she locked the door behind her.

"Buongiorno! Ciao! Hello," I said cheerfully, attempting to look nonchalant and not as if I'd been standing there eavesdropping. "How are you today?"

She just nodded again and walked away, leaving me feeling like an idiot. Which is not a new thing. I shrugged and watch her leave, heading down the narrow passageway into the darkening city.

CHAPTER FOURTEEN

The evening passed without incident. I checked my emails – no reply yet from Charlie. Wrote a bit more of the book, the story starting to bear more and more resemblance to what was actually going on here (which was certainly strange enough to negate the need for me to make anything up). Watched an old Woody Allen movie (in English) on the TV, picking at the tasty bits and pieces of food I'd picked up from the supermarket.

Another text message from Will – this time with more kisses at the end – wishing me goodnight (my heart melted a little bit more...).

I wrote into the night, the story finally coming together in my head. It was the story of a writer, in Venice to cure her writer's block, who falls in love and becomes embroiled in a murder investigation...

I didn't know yet how it was going to end, but the beginning was certainly exciting.

I went to bed about 2.00am, and had just tumbled into bed

when I heard a loud noise outside. I leapt up and ran out into the living room, listening out for sounds of distress from upstairs again; but it was only my elderly female neighbour coming home. I smiled to myself; here was I, a successful, wealthy, single woman in her (*middle-age*) prime, standing around in my nightie, while the old dear upstairs was out partying. Even a crazy geriatric had more of a social life than I did.

I was woken just after 6.00am by my phone ringing. *Who on earth could be ringing me at this ungodly hour?*

It was Will.

"Hey Will..." I yawned, still half asleep.

"I'm sorry to call you so early," he said, urgently. "But there's been another one..."

I rushed through the streets, following the Map app on my phone to the address Will had given me. It was a large square, lined with cafes, a church at one end and several souvenir shops, one of which was cordoned off with police tape.

Will was waiting anxiously behind the tape, looking out for me. He smiled when he saw me approach carrying two takeaway coffees.

"Here," I said, handing him one. "I thought you could probably use this."

He took it gratefully and lifted the tape so I could duck under.

I felt just like a character in an American TV cop show. *CSI Venice!*

"Thank you," he said. "In here."

The shop, Carlevaro's, was one of the many in Venice that made and sold carnival masks. Carnival is a BIG THING in Venice, and masks are everywhere. In the doorway a full-size mannequin, dressed in robes and wearing a plague doctor's mask with a long, curved beak-like nose, stood on guard. Inside the shop was dark, the small windows swathed in heavy red velvet and the walls painted a rich deep blue. Any surface that could be gilded, was. Gold gleamed, mirrors twinkled and a magnificent chandelier hung from the ceiling, casting shadows upon the masks ranged along the shelves. Some of them were bona fide works of art, hand-painted and beautifully coloured; while others were just plain creepy. Through the windows, I could see locals and tourists starting to gather out in the square beyond the police tape, trying to peer in at the crime scene.

———

"Wow," I said, as Will led me through the shop. "This place is incredible! And a little bit tacky."

He grinned. "Thought you'd like it," he said, as we reached a door at the back of the shop. "Not sure what you'll make of this though. Don't touch anything."

He nodded at the police officer on the door, who opened it and stood aside to let us in.

The first thing that hit me was the smell. *Shit!* Literally. A really strong smell of shit, mingled with something else; something sharp, almost metallic.

The second thing that hit me was the dead man stretched out against the wall.

The room was a workshop – Carlevaro's ran mask-making classes for tourists – with a couple of large workbenches and chairs, a notice board with drawings of customers' designs pinned to it, and boxes of materials:sequins, paints, feathers. A couple of adjustable spotlights sat on the benches, presumably to allow the mask-makers to see their creations better; but now they were both pointed at the far wall, illuminating the dead man.

Arms outstretched, crucifix-like, and bound with ropes stretched cruelly tight to keep him upright, he sagged nonetheless between them, head thrown back. That was where the metallic smell was coming from; the long thin gash in his neck was crusted with blood, which also covered his clothes and the wall in front of him. I guessed his carotid artery had been cut.

I didn't have to look too hard to discover the source of the shitty smell.

"Oh my god!" I stammered, holding onto Will. He grabbed my arm to steady me.

The victim's trousers and underwear had been pulled down to reveal his arse. And another plague doctor's mask – with the long, thin beak – had been inserted up it. Quite a long way up it, by the look of things.

""That's horrible!" I said, unable to take my eyes off it.

"I know," said Will.

"I mean, who would put peacock feathers and leopard skin print on the same mask?" I could see Will regarding me with a slightly shocked look on his face. I wobbled (even more than usual) and he sat me down on a chair.

"Sorry," I said. "That was hugely inappropriate. I appear to have developed stress-related Tourettes."

"Don't worry about it," he reassured me. "It's a coping mechanism. Doctors and nurses, emergency workers, they often develop a sick sense of humour to get them through the nasty stuff. You have to laugh or you'll go mad."

That was it exactly.

"So, how did the murderer enter? In through the back door?" I asked, innocently. We both snorted with suppressed hysteria at that one. "Oh my god, I just can't help myself..." I apologised.

"Che cazzo fa qui?" A furious barrage of Italian hit us. I turned around guiltily to see Manera standing there, looking at me like he'd quite happily insert a carnival mask into one of *my* orifices.

"Good morning, Inspector Manera," I said super politely, but he ignored me and glared at Will who looked stubbornly back.

"Inspector," he said calmly. "I did tell you yesterday that I was bringing another consultant onto the case."

"A consultant, *si!* Not a fucking *narratore!*"

Will took a deep breath.

"Interpol use many different types of consultants, and in a case like this we need someone who can see into the mind of a crazed murderer, who can think like the kind of homicidal maniac who can commit terrible crimes without a second thought for the humanity of the victim or the merest drop of compassion for their suffering. Someone who delights in brutality and imaginative torture." Will sounded very pleased with that little speech and I imagined him rehearsing it for just such an occasion.

"That'll be me, then!" I said lightly. And then thought about what he'd actually just said about me. "Oh, right..." Will grinned and winked at me as Manera looked around the room.

"Agent Carmichael..." Manera clearly wasn't convinced and took Will to one side, where they spoke in hushed but urgent tones, about me obviously. I tried and failed not to look at the carnival mask lodged in the victim's anus while they argued, which wasn't a thing I'd expected to be doing on my holidays.

Finally the Inspector threw up his hands in the International Sign Language gesture for 'have it your own way but you're making a huge mistake and don't come crying to me when it all goes to shit'. He glared at me.

"Ok, Signora Creative Consultant, what kind of mad man do you think committed such a crime?" he spat out.

I shrugged. "I just got here. Fuck knows."

Will snorted with another suppressed laugh as the Inspector glared at me again (he was an Olympic-standard glarer), huffed and stormed out. Will looked at me, half reproachful, half in admiration, I wasn't sure why.

"Fuck nose!" he said, miming the shape of the hooked beak of the offending carnival mask and sniggering.

"That was completely unintentional, I swear!" I protested, giggling nervously, hysteria bubbling just under the surface again.

"Oh stop it, this is so unprofessional!" Will looked away from me and composed himself. He frowned. "Does that notice board look odd to you?' he asked, pointing to the large pin board that covered most of one wall. I walked over and studied it closely while Will ran his hands over it.

"Not really –" As I spoke, Will found a handle on one side of the notice board and pulled. The whole thing swung backwards; a hidden door. He looked at me, eyebrows raised. "Holy crap, you're good!" I said. "Did you read the Famous Five as a child?"

Behind the door was a dark chamber. I began to step through but he threw his arm across my chest to stop me. "Wait there!"

Tentatively Will entered the room beyond, fumbling around for a light switch. A bright light flicked on and I heard him swear. "Oh shit."

I followed him in and stopped in shock.

In the middle of the room was a bed, with a camera on a tripod and some movie lights set up next to it. In one corner, a desk with a computer and monitor.

I looked at the bed, its sheets crumpled and soiled, and shivered. I didn't want to imagine what had gone on there. Will approached the computer and jiggled the mouse; the monitor sprang to life. He gulped.

"What is it?" I asked. Will didn't answer. He reached out and pressed a key on the keyboard. Immediately the sound of a man talking in a soft, persuasive voice floated towards me, followed by crying. The crying sounded horribly like that of a young boy.

"Fucking hell, Will, what is that?" I rushed over to the desk but he quickly pressed another key, stopping the footage. He grabbed me and steered me out of the room.

"Trust me, you don't want to see it."

"But –"

"No, Bella!" He steered me all the way out into the shop, stopping to say a few words to the police officer on the door to the workshop, who looked stunned for a few seconds before talking into his radio.

A team of forensic officers entered the shop, carrying

equipment cases. Will spoke briefly to them before grabbing me by the arm again and gently but firmly leading me outside.

We left the square and Carlevaro's shop behind us and headed towards the nearby Rialto Bridge, where Will finally stopped and sank into a chair outside a café.

He looked grey-faced. I reached across the table and took his hand.

"Was that footage on the computer – was that what I think it was?" I asked gently. He nodded.

"And our murder victim – was that his voice?"

"I don't know," said Will, signalling to the waiter and ordering two café lattes.

"Who was he? The shop owner?"

"Yes." Will nodded. "Roberto Carlevaro. The Carlevaro family have had a shop on that site for hundreds of years, almost as long as they've celebrated *Carnevale* here. Roberto was arrested a year or so ago on a charge of lewd behaviour, but it never got to court."

"What the bloody hell's 'lewd behaviour' when it's at home?" I asked.

Will shrugged. "I'm not sure. It could cover anything from exposing himself in a public place to propositioning another man in a toilet –"

"What about propositioning a woman?" I asked, indignantly. Will allowed himself a smile at that.

"This is Italy. Propositioning women is a way of life..."

"Thank God you're British, then," I said. "I wouldn't feel safe otherwise."

He laughed and reached across the table to hold my other hand.

"Last night –" he began, stopping as the waiter brought our coffee.

"Grazie." I thanked the waiter and watched him leave, then smiled at Will. "It's all right, I know you were busy. I keep forgetting you actually have to work now and again."

We sipped our coffee and gazed across the Grand Canal for a moment, watching the *vaparetto* boats going up and down the waterway.

"At least we know why he was killed," I said. Will looked up in surprise.

"We do?"

"How much crime – violent crime, anyway – does Venice have? Not much, I'm betting."

"No," said Will. "Apart from petty crimes like pick-pocketing, it's very safe."

"So it's highly unlikely that we've suddenly got two murderers turning up within a few days of each other, isn't it? Particularly two such gruesome and creative murderers."

"Well yes, I would say it's fairly safe to assume that whoever murdered Gerbasi on Poveglia is probably the same person who killed Carlevaro last night," said Will.

"And we think that Gerbasi was a paedophile –"

"Conjecture at this stage, but yes."

"And we know that Carlevaro was."

"If that was his voice in the footage," said Will. I looked at him, exasperated. He held up his hand to stop me talking. "I know, I know, it was in a secret room in his shop. I think you're probably right, Bella, I'm just saying that we shouldn't discount other possibilities until we know that's the connection. We should at least consider other angles, if only to rule them out."

I laughed, humourlessly. "Perhaps the devil came to claim his soul."

Will looked puzzled. "Pardon me?"

"I read this story last night," I told him. "Funnily enough, it was in the same book where I first heard about Poveglia..."

The Mask Maker and The Devil

In the early days of the *Carnevale,* there was an artist who was very poor. He was extremely talented but his family were of such low birth that no one would buy his paintings.

One day, the Devil came to him and asked the artist to make him a mask; he wanted to visit the carnival, but God wouldn't let him anywhere near it. The artist made a mask of such beauty that the Devil was able to fool God and attend the city's masked ball on the last night.

After that, every year the Devil would appear to the artist and order a mask for the ball; and every year, he would make him a mask that outshone all the others at *carnevale.* The artist grew very rich and successful, and all the noble families who had previously looked down on him now insisted on buying their masks from him alone.

And then one year, the artist surpassed himself with the Devil's mask; it was the most beautiful creation anyone had ever seen. But the day before the Devil was due to collect it, a nobleman came to the artist's workshop with his youngest daughter, whose beauty was greater than that of all the other girls in Venice. The artist could not tear his eyes away from her, and when she saw the Devil's mask and asked her father to buy it for her, he could not refuse.

As soon as the girl and her father left the artist's workshop, the Devil appeared, and told him in a furious rage that he must get back the mask, or replace it with one that was even more beautiful.

The artist ran to the nobleman's house and begged the girl to give the mask back; but her father would not hear of it. The terrified man waited in his workshop, surrounded by his other masks, which were all beautiful and life-like but none so much as the one he'd sold. When the Devil appeared at midnight, he flew into a fury and demanded to know where the mask was, but the artist, who truly loved the nobleman's daughter, refused to tell him. The Devil clicked his fingers and the masks in the studio came to life, one by one; and one by one they drained the life force from the unfortunate man.

The Devil meanwhile still needed a mask, so he went out into the streets to look for one, where he came upon the nobleman's daughter. He too was taken with her beauty; so taken that he decided to tear her face off and use it as his mask.

Will grimaced as I finished talking.

"Good grief, woman, where did you get that horrible story from?"

"I told you, I have this book." I sipped at my coffee. The old tale had made my mouth dry. "It's full of spooky old legends set in Venice. Someone sent me it."

"Well maybe the killer's read it too," said Will. "They seem to know the stories, anyway."

I shuddered.

"I bloody well hope not!" I cried. "There are twenty five stories in that book! I don't mind writing about serial killers but I wouldn't want to meet one."

Will laughed and reached across the table to touch my hand again.

"Don't worry, you're safe with me," he said, smiling. I felt all warm and fuzzy for a moment, but then a thought struck me.

"It's weird actually," I said slowly. "But that book – it wasn't where I'd left it. And it was open at the beginning of that story, about the mask maker –"

Will laughed. "Do you think the killer's communicating with you through a book? You probably just left it there while you were getting ready and didn't realise you had."

"Hmmm..."

I clearly wasn't convinced, because he frowned. "Bella, do you seriously think that someone's been in your apartment? Because I can come and check the locks and secure everything if you do."

I shook my head, suddenly feeling stupid.

"No, no, you're right. I was probably in the middle of something and just picked it up without thinking. There was no sign of any break in, and the front door's a big heavy lump of wood with a massive iron lock on it, so..."

He squeezed my hand. "Well, if you *are* worried, tell me and I'll have a good look at your apartment and make sure it's all safe."

We sat for a while, just drinking and mulling things over, then he shook himself.

"I really should go. I get the feeling Manera hasn't finished with me yet for bringing you along."

"If it's going to cause you trouble –" I began, hoping that he wouldn't say yes it would, because despite the horrific things I'd seen so far working with him wasn't just clearing my writer's block, it was absolutely obliterating it into tiny pieces. And, of course, I was just enjoying being with him.

"I like trouble," he grinned.

I mentally slapped myself round the face as my heart did a pathetic girly flutter.

"I was so hoping you'd say that!"

CHAPTER FIFTEEN

I spent the rest of the day writing. It's amazing how a gruesome and spectacularly nasty murder can get the creative juices flowing (or is that just me? I hope it's not just me). The words flew from my fingertips, and I'd gone from not knowing what to say – just plonking any old shite down onto the page – to not being able to type fast enough to keep up with my brain.

Some writers are planners; they write a detailed outline of the story; then they write biographies for the main characters – even (in some cases) down to where they went to school, the name of their first pet and their favourite type of biscuit (which, incidentally, if you put those last two together equals your stripper stage-name). Then they write a list of all the scenes, or chapters, and what happens in each one...

Other writers just jump straight in and write the bloody thing.

Guess which school I belong to?

But this time I knew exactly where this story was going, even allowing for the fact that I was allowing real-life events to influence it. I knew what was happening three chapters ahead, I could see the ending (a little blurrily, but it was there). I KNEW that the female lead would end up jumping the male lead because he was too shy to get on with it, but when she eventually did, he would respond whole-heartedly and with great gusto...

That made me need a cold drink.

In short – I wrote like a woman possessed. Or more accurately, a woman so sexually frustrated she needed an outlet to take her mind off it.

Susie rang. Whereas in London she'd had the unnerving knack of ringing me just after I'd deleted an entire week's work, here she kept interrupting me in full flow.

I declined the call, felt guilty, started to dial her number and then changed my mind. I needed another drink.

I walked through to the kitchen with my glass and stopped, dropping the glass in shock when I spotted Francesca's book next to the kettle. I DEFINITELY hadn't left it there.

Or had I? No, I hadn't. But –

"Oh for fuck's sake!" I said out loud. "If there's the ghost of a long-dead librarian in here who keeps moving my book around to try and make me put it away, will you just stop it? You're really starting to piss me off now."

I often talk to myself and I occasionally wonder what I'd do if someone actually replied. Thankfully, that's never happened. And it didn't this time, either. I shook my head at my own stupidity; of course I'd moved the book myself, I'd been writing for hours and when I wasn't, I was thinking about my story or the murders or Will – it would be so easy for me to absentmindedly move something and not even notice I was doing it.

I swore at myself and dropped to my knees to sweep up the broken glass, cutting my finger in the process. I grabbed a tea towel and wrapped it around my bleeding digit, then poked around in the kitchen cupboards and drawers for a plaster.

I found a box of Band Aids and sorted out my wound (*tiny cut, you wimp*) but as I replaced the box, my fingers touched something else at the back of the drawer. I pulled it out.

It was a passport. It was Francesca's, and it was still in date. I frowned to myself. Francesca was in Australia, so how could her passport be here?

I studied it closely – I don't know why, it's not like it could tell me why it was still here in Venice and not on the other side of the world – and looked at Francesca's photograph. She wasn't the old Italian grandma I'd imagined, but a much younger, handsome woman in her late 50s, with a striking mass of dark, curly hair.

I took the passport back to the desk and found Francesca's email address. As I typed her an email, it struck me that I had no idea who she really was. Maybe she was a spy or a drug trafficker or – or - *an international woman of mystery!!!* Maybe she had more than one passport – maybe she travelled under different identities, doing nefarious deeds across the globe...

Maybe I was being stupid and getting carried away.

I deleted the email, unsure of what I'd actually been about to write anyway, and checked my inbox; still nothing from Charlie, my contact at the school. He'd probably moved on somewhere else, or he'd changed his email. I'd known it was a long shot, and there was no guarantee that he'd have found anything, anyway.

There was a knock on the door. I went and answered it and found Will on the doorstep, smiling.

"Sorry I had to abandon you earlier," he said.

"It's fine, you had to work." I opened the door wider and stepped back to let him in, but he stayed on the doorstep.

"I came to invite you to a picnic."

"When?"

"Now."

"But it's dark..."

"Best time," he grinned. "It'll be less crowded."

I grabbed my shoes and bag – slipping Francesca's passport inside, as an idea occurred to me – and we headed out into the street.

We wandered through dark and winding back streets until I was so lost I couldn't tell right from left or up from down.

"Lost yet?" Will grinned at me.

"Only completely," I said.

"Then you are now a true Venetian!" he declared. "Seriously, getting lost in Venice at night is a rite of passage. Even life-long residents get lost in the dark."

"You're not lost though, are you?" I said. "I can't imagine you ever getting lost anywhere."

He laughed. "Don't you believe it. My first week here, I'd found my way around the whole city without putting a foot wrong. I was starting to get a little bit smug that I hadn't done what everyone else supposedly does. I thought they must be fools to get lost so easily. And then I went out to eat in the Rialto district that night and got so confused I had to hire a water taxi to take me home."

"That doesn't sound so bad –"

"This was after I'd walked around in circles for two hours. When I told the boatman where I wanted to go, he looked at me like I was mad but said ok."

"And...?"

"And then took me around the next corner and stopped right outside my house." I laughed and he took my arm to guide me up some dark stone stairs onto a bridge. I stopped for a moment and looked down at the black water. Behind us, moonlight streamed through a gap in the buildings, silhouetting our reflections on the surface of the canal. I turned to Will and he leaned in to kiss me, tenderly. *Swoon.*

"Come on," he said. "Come and meet the other woman in my life."

The what? My heart leapt but I didn't speak and held onto his hand as we walked on.

We crossed a square, lined with shops – second-hand books, antiques, glass – and cafes, which during the day would no doubt have spilled out into the street, but now were closed and silent. Lights shone in the windows of the apartments above, but it was very quiet – just the sound of our footsteps. And something else.

A high pitched cry of distress, from the tree in the centre of the square.

We stopped and looked up into the branches. Two tiny glowing eyes peered down at us, trapped in a ball of fur. A kitten sat in the tree, mewing pathetically.

"Do you think it's trapped?" I asked. Will nodded.

"Daft animals, cats," he said. He climbed onto the bench underneath the tree, perfectly placed to take advantage of the shade during the heat of the day and for rescuing kittens at night, and reached up into the branches. The kitten struggled but he talked to it softly.

"*Calmati, piccolino!* It's ok, little one," he cooed. He freed the kitten and climbed down, holding it close to his face and talking to it. "See? You're free."

I watched him stroking the little bundle of fluff, the kitten mewing back in reply, and felt my insides go all squiffy. *Oh. My. God. If this man ever holds a baby in front of me, my ovaries are toast.*

I reached out and stroked the cat in his hands, and smiling, he turned to me.

"What are the odds the daft creature goes straight back up the tree the moment I let her go?" he said. He put the kitten down and sure enough...

We laughed and walked on, leaving the furry siren there to tempt other passersby into rescuing and making a fuss of her.

"Nearly there," said Will. We walked along another narrow passageway, across a small stone bridge, and then turned onto a much longer wooden one. This canal was a lot wider than the others, and it was very dark – just the reflection of a few house lights on the water. He took my hand again and led me across.

"Where are we going?" I asked, halfway across. He pointed out to the water.

"Down there."

We carried on walking, then at the end turned onto a waterside pathway.

"Careful along here," he said. "It's very dark."

No shit...

"Right, here we go," he said, letting go of my hand. "Just wait there a moment..."

He stepped onto a narrow jetty and disappeared from view. Then ...

"Ta da!" he cried. Lights appeared, hundreds of fairy lights and lanterns draped around a boat. In the middle of the boat a table and two chairs had been set up, and they too were surrounded by tiny lights, twinkling, reflecting in the water so it looked like they were adrift in an ocean of stars.

"Wow!" I cried. "It's lovely. Is this your boat?"

"Yep!" said Will, proudly. "*La Sirena.* The only other woman in my life. Come aboard!"

He held out his hand as I wobbled onto the boat and sat down. The *Sirena* wasn't very big – there wasn't much room around the table – but she looked sturdy enough to my eyes.

Will reached under the table and brought out a basket. "Would madam care for some refreshments?" he said. "There's a bottle of wine under the table too, if I didn't just kick it over. I had this vision in my head of what this would look like...I think I needed a bigger boat..."

I laughed. "Don't worry about the wine, the food looks lovely. It all looks lovely."

Will started to lay out food on the table.

"And here we have a selection of the finest cold meats and local cheeses..."

"Honestly, you should quit Interpol and become a waiter," I teased.

He pretended to mull it over. "Well, I did think about it, but being a secret agent has better hours. And of course the ladies all love an international super spy..."

"Do we?" I asked.

"Don't you? Shit..."

He found the wine – it was still upright, after all – and poured two glasses. He raised his in a toast and then stopped.

"What shall we drink to?" he asked.

"To being right here, right now," I said. He smiled.

"I wouldn't want to be anywhere else," he said.

We drank.

"So how did you end up being an international super spy?" I said.

He laughed. "Why, are you thinking of a career change?"

"No seriously, how did you end up in Interpol? I'm interested. I want to know all about you."

"I was in the Army. Spent some time in Military Intelligence, so Interpol or MI6 was the logical next step."

"Why did you leave the Army?" He frowned. "Sorry, I'm being nosey. You don't have to tell me."

"No, no it's fine," he said, but he didn't look like it was fine. "I was discharged."

"Why?"

He sighed. "You're not very good at taking hints, are you?"

"I'm sorry," I said. "Ignore me, you don't have to tell me." *But please do because I'm really intrigued now.*

"Ok. I was discharged because I assaulted a superior officer." He smiled grimly. "Actually I take that back. He might have been a higher rank than me, but that man wasn't superior to anyone."

I was stunned. "What do you mean, assaulted?"

"I believe the civilian term for it is 'I kicked the shit out of him'."

I was shocked. I didn't like to (and couldn't) imagine Will fighting with anybody, but maybe I was being naïve. He was a soldier, after all.

"What happened?"

He took a long drink from his wine glass and looked at me. "I'm not proud of what happened," he said. "But at the same time, in the same circumstances I'd do it again.

"It was at a regimental dinner. A typically smug, self-congratulatory affair. I always much preferred eating with the lads in the mess, but once you get past a certain rank you have to go to a few of these things otherwise you're considered to not be a team player. My commanding officer, a particularly self-satisfied piece of shit, got drunk as he always did and started to get handy with the waiting staff. He was infamous for it. Bastard.

"But there was a new waitress that night. She only looked about fifteen, although she must've been older. He wouldn't leave her alone. It was getting awkward. Eventually the dinner ended and he said he was going to the kitchen to congratulate the chef on a wonderful meal, but we all knew what he was doing."

He looked at the reflection of the fairy lights in the water.

"I snapped. I followed him outside and found him. He'd pinned the poor girl against the wall and had his hand up her skirt. She was terrified. I tapped him on the shoulder and as soon as he turned around, wham! I punched him in the face."

"Good!" I said. He smiled.

"It did feel good," he said. "Until the MPs came and arrested me."

"Were you court-martialled?" I asked.

"No," he said. "The top brass knew what he was like, and they wanted to keep it quiet. He was forced to drop all charges against me, but in return I had to leave. At least I left with my record and my good name intact. In fact, another of the officers put in a word for me with a contact at Interpol."

"And the rest is history."

"Yes. "

He looked at me with a resigned expression on his face, like now I knew the truth about him I'd hightail it out of there or something. I smiled at him in an attempt to bring the earlier mood back. "So what's an international super spy of your calibre doing in Venice? It's not known for being a hive of criminal activity, is it?" I paused. "At least, it wasn't til I got here."

"Is that a confession?" he laughed. The mood was back... "No, Venice is a very safe place. Usually. Interpol sent me here to consult with the local police on possible Mafia activity."

"Oooh how exciting!" I squealed, spilling my wine.

"Not really, as it turns out. The Italians have really cracked down on the crime families and organised gangs in recent years, particularly in their traditional strongholds like Naples and Sicily. But there were fears that this was just moving the problem on to quieter places, where the police were perhaps less likely to notice what they were up to."

"You thought the Mafia had opened up here?" I was intrigued.

"We had intelligence that the son of one of the big Sicilian families was planning to move to Venice and set up shop in the Canneregio district. So I came along to keep an eye on him."

"And did he?"

"Yes, he did move, and yes, he did set up shop. A cheese shop."

"A cheese shop? What was it, a cover for selling drugs, or laundering money, or –"

"No, it was a shop for selling cheese." Will grinned as I looked at him in astonishment and burst out laughing. "Honestly, he just sells cheese. Of course, I didn't know that at first and I had to keep going in there to check on him. And now I'm his best customer. I've become something of an expert on cheese. Go on, ask me about cheese. Anything you like."

I giggled. "Ok. What's the best cheese for luring a bear out of a cave?"

He looked at me, eyebrows raised.

"Camembert," I said. Silence. "You get it? Cam – on – bear...cam on..."

He paused for a moment, then guffawed so loudly the boat rocked and a dog barked in a house nearby.

"Oh that's terrible," he laughed. We both got the giggles then, Will wiping at his eyes. "Seriously, that is the worst joke I've ever heard," he said.

"Oh I've got much worse than that!" I cried, and he laughed even harder.

We finally calmed down. He took my hand, smiling across the table at me.

"Oh Bella, Bella...you're so clever and funny and beautiful, why hasn't some lucky man snapped you up? Can't you cook?"

He ducked as I pulled my hand away to slap him and put his own in front of his face for protection, laughing.

"I'm joking, I'm joking! Please don't push me off the boat..."

"Just watch it, Agent Carmichael!" I warned. "And actually, a lucky man did snap me up, but..."

I met Joel, the bastard unfaithful ex-husband as he was to become, at a book awards ceremony. The Smoking Gun awards are held every year to celebrate the work of murderers, thieves and despots (or 'crime writers', as we're otherwise known). Modesty prevents me from reporting who is the current holder of the most Smoking Gun trophies for Best Crime Fiction Novel (Oh all right, it's me!), but the year I met Joel, competition for it had been particularly fierce.

I sat in the audience with Susie and her husband/boss Guy (nepotism is rife in publishing...), and applauded the winners, commiserated with the losers, and waited impatiently to hear if I'd won. Again.

The MC handed over the trophy - a polished chrome gun, smoke curling from its barrel – for Best Crime Non-Fiction, and moved on.

"And the winner of this year's Smoking Gun award for Best Crime Fiction is –" I braced myself – "- the new enfant terrible of murder most foul, Joel Quigley!"

Bollocks! I plastered on a smile – ha ha ha, yes, so pleased for him, he really deserved it - *talentless bell-end* – as the terrible infant made his way onto the stage. He raised the trophy high, his gaze sweeping the crowd, eyes resting mockingly on me for a moment before moving on.

I excused myself and went to the bar, and stayed there. I might be a sore loser, but at least I'm magnanimous in victory.

Half an hour later, the bar was full. Joel stood in the middle of the room, holding court to the bevy (I use that word advisedly, as most of them had had a few beverages by then) of vacuous blondes who were hanging on to his every word and laughing at all his jokes (and honestly, his jokes were even worse than mine). He looked over at me as I turned and caught his eye. I raised my glass to him and turned away.

Thirty seconds later he was by my side.

"We haven't met. You're Annabelle Tyson, aren't you?" he said.

"Please, Bella. Only my mum and my publisher call me Annabelle."

"Ok, Bella. I'm –"

"I know who you are," I interrupted him. "Your name's on your trophy."

He smiled drunkenly and lifted it up (he was still holding it! who does that?), reading the engraving on the front.

"Oh, yeah, so it does."

"I know that because, you see, I won one of them last year."

"I know."

"And the year before that. And the –" Ok, this wasn't my finest witty exchange with a man, but it had been a long and slightly disappointing night and I was full of Sauvignon Blanc.

"I get it, you're a brilliant writer. I know you are. Can this year's winner buy last year's winner a drink, or shall we just skip to the part where I shag you in the toilets?"

Charming!

"I think one trophy's enough for tonight," I said, patting him on the shoulder. "But you can get me that drink."

So he bought me another glass of wine, and then another, and later on he persuaded me to go back to his cheap hotel room (admittedly he didn't have to do that much persuading, but at least I avoided the toilets – I have *standards*, you know). However it wasn't just a one night stand - we met at another awards ceremony a month or so later and repeated the whole thing again (even down to him beating me to a statuette). A two night stand!

We started seeing each other properly after that, and found that we actually liked each other even away from awards ceremonies, alcohol and dodgy hotels.

Two months later he moved in.

By the time the next Smoking Gun awards rolled around, we were married. He was younger and hotter than me, and he fancied the arse off me! I wasn't about to let go of that. And we made each other laugh, we talked about writing, we watched movies together... When it was my turn to win the award that year, he kissed me and watched proudly as I went on stage to collect it. We thought about celebrating by revisiting the Travelodge for a nostalgic bunk up but he'd booked a swanky hotel nearby, and we managed to keep our hands off each other just about long enough to get back to our room (although we did make a start in the cab).

The next year he smiled and raised a glass to me, but there was no hotel, cheap, swanky or otherwise.

Two years later and the smile had disappeared, along with what was left of his writing career. And the year after that, when I got up on stage and squinted into the audience I saw his seat was empty.

I went out to find him in the bar, just in time to see him leaving the toilets with a young, scantily clad brunette, who was adjusting her clothing. She obviously had lower standards than me.

I gave him another chance. Maybe it was my fault? I'd been so busy with my career, maybe I'd neglected him? I didn't think I had, but he somehow managed to convince me that he was the victim in all this. My success seemed to be in direct correlation with his failure, but really, his first book had been such a massive success (much more so than my early ones) that anything that followed had a hard time competing against it. Expectations – his fans', his publisher's and particularly his own – were so high, they were doomed to be disappointed.

So I let him stay.

And he ended up screwing the barmaid at our local pub in return. I'm pretty sure there were others, but I could never prove it.

Our marriage lasted five years, five months and seventeen days. And in the two years since, his career had taken off like a rocket again while mine had stopped in its tracks, so who knows? Maybe it was my fault.

"He turned out to be a bit of a shit," I paraphrased. Will shook his head.

"What an idiot."

I smiled. "Anyway, what about you? Is there a Mrs Carmichael hidden away in an attic somewhere?"

Will had just raised his glass to take a drink. He choked mid-sip. I looked at him in concern but he just coughed, swallowed and then smiled.

"I'm fine, it's just what happens every time I think about my ex-wife," he croaked. "Have you heard that famous Paul Newman quote, when someone asked him how he'd managed to have such a long and happy marriage, particularly in a place like Hollywood?" I shook my head. "He said, 'why go out for a hamburger when you've got steak at home?'"

I was mystified. "And...?"

Will smiled, matter of factly. "Turns out my ex-wife loved hamburgers." He reached out and grabbed something out of the basket, holding it up suggestively. "Salami?"

Wine finished, food consumed, we weaved our way slightly unsteadily back through the streets towards Francesca's apartment, talking animatedly. Well, I talked, Will listened, occasionally shaking his head and laughing at me.

"And then I said –" I flung my arms out dramatically (*drunkenly*), almost throwing myself off balance and knocking Will into a canal. He grabbed me and laughed as I clutched onto him. "My hero!"

We stood there for a moment, laughter subsiding as we clung onto each other tightly. I rested my head on his shoulder, thankful that he was 5'6" and not 6'2", as otherwise I'd have been resting my head on his stomach, and giggled again.

He smiled. "What's so funny?"

"Nothing! I was just thinking, you're the perfect height for me... I could stand here and snog you for ages without getting a neck ache..."

"Hmmm...I like your theory but without proof –" I cut him off with a quick peck on the mouth.

He tenderly took my face in my hands and gazed into my eyes, then our lips met softly.

It turned out my theory was correct.

We finally made it back to Francesca's apartment. I searched for my keys, then turned to Will.

"Um – would you like to come in?" I asked, suddenly feeling very nervous.

He took my hands and smiled at me.

"I'd love to –"

'But?" It came out a bit harsher than I intended. I looked away. "Sorry, I'd didn't mean it to sound quite like that. But we've had such a lovely night –"

"Yes, we have!" said Will, quickly. "Which is why I don't want to rush things."

Just my luck – I pushed that thought away. It was sweet, really.

"I have this habit of jumping in too quick," he carried on. "And then it all goes wrong, and we both get hurt –"

"This won't go wrong!" I blurted. *Jesus Christ, woman, how desperate do you sound?* "I mean – I really like you –"

"And I really like you," he smiled. "I'm not going anywhere, are you? So why hurry?"

Because I'm going to EXPLODE!

"You're right," I sighed. He smiled and drew me close.

"Can I have that in writing?" he asked. "Women don't say that very often, in my experience..."

"Two sexist comments in one night?" I said, in mock indignation. "That's it, your invitation's been revoked."

He leaned in to kiss me goodnight, and by the time he finished I'd forgiven him.

We finally said our goodbyes, and as he turned to leave I remembered the passport I'd discovered earlier.

"Wait!" I said, searching my bag for it. "Here. I found this today."

Will put out his hand to take it. "What is it?"

"Francesca's passport." He pulled back his hand as if something had bitten it.

"Where did you get that?" he asked. I hiccupped and tasted prosecco.

"Oops! Pardon me. I found it in the back of the kitchen drawer. But if Francesca's in Australia, what's her passport doing here?"

"It's probably an old one," said Will, dismissively. I shook my head.

"No, it's not expired. I wondered – what with you being an international super spy and all –"

"Do you want me to look up Francesca's whereabouts and see if she's ok?" he asked.

"Can you do that? Is that ok?"

"It's fine," he said. "She probably just couldn't find it and got a new one, but if it puts your mind at rest I'll double check."

"Thanks, babe," I said, kicking myself as I realised what I'd called him. But he smiled. "You're welcome. So don't worry about it, or Francesca. I have to go, but I'll see you tomorrow. Lunch?"

"Sounds good."

One last quick kiss, then I leant sleepily (*drunkenly*) against the doorframe and watched him disappear into the night.

I was so tired, I just about managed to clean my teeth and change into my pyjamas before I fell asleep.

CHAPTER SIXTEEN

D r Gerbasi was waiting for me in the shadow of the bell tower again, his head lolling even more now. I wondered whether I should point out that it was in danger of completely parting company with his body, but decided against it. I hated him but at the same time, as my old gran used to say, if you can't say anything nice, don't say anything at all. I am British, you know. Manners are important.

"I suppose you don't care who killed me now," he said, his voice taking on a wheedling, self-pitying tone.

"You mean now I know you were a kiddie fiddler?" I said angrily.

"Don't judge me!" he said, but weakly; he knew he was fighting a losing battle here. I'd already judged him, and the part of me that wasn't a confirmed atheist hoped that mine wasn't the only judgement he'd face. And that the next one would involve fire, brimstone and pitchforks up the arse.

"You shouldn't wish that upon anybody!" said Roberto Carlevaro, who I suddenly noticed was standing next to me. He looked a little awkward loitering there, with his shirt front stiff with dried blood and his backside full of carnival mask. Gerbasi shifted over to make room for him on the rusty bed-frame he was sitting on.

"Here you go, *amico*," he said. "Take the weight off."

Carlevaro started to sit down, then straightened up abruptly. "No, I'm good thanks."

"Why do you keep bothering me?" I asked Gerbasi, trying not to notice the fly that was crawling towards his mouth.

"Avenge my death!" he said, waving his arms about in a Jacob Marley fashion, rattling the length of chain around his neck.

"Get fucked!" I snorted incredulously. I couldn't believe the sheer bloody cheek of it. Avenge his death? I'd be more likely to shake the hand of the murderer and congratulate him or her on a job well done.

"See?" Gerbasi turned to Carlevaro. "I told you, she doesn't care."

"If it's that obvious, why do you keep luring me here?" I asked.

"How would we know? We're not the ones doing the luring ," said Gerbasi indignantly.

"Yeah, right. Then who is?" I asked.

Carlevaro pointed up at the bell tower, where just like last time, someone twisted and turned high in the air. I tensed, not wanting to see Will hanging there, contorted and blue in the face, but unable to not look.

It wasn't Will. It was me.

I jumped awake, gasping for breath, hands reaching up to my neck to tug at the thick metal chain that had wrapped itself around me in the dark – but of course it wasn't there. I stuck out a hand and turned on the bedside lamp, but the small pool of light it shed served only to heighten the shadows in the corner of the room.

Pull yourself together! I told myself sternly, forcing my legs out of the bed; my feet tensing as they touched the cold tile floor, waiting for a rough hand to reach out from under the bed and drag me down. But it didn't. *Of course. Idiot!*

I went out to the kitchen and drank a glass of cold water. Noises from above; didn't the old lady ever bloody sleep? I was getting fed up with hearing her arguing and stomping about, shrieking in the middle of the night with her bad dreams.

There was definitely someone up there with her this time, though. I could only hear one side of the conversation – the old lady certainly had a big mouth on her – but I could also just about make out the low murmur of a reply. Whoever he was (I felt certain it was a he – something about the pitch of those murmurs), he was much calmer than she was; she was gabbling away loudly, an accusatory tone in her voice, while he tried to placate her. Then the tears started.

I stood frozen to the spot, listening. It went quiet. I listened for a while but there was nothing. I relaxed, only then noticing how tense I was, and headed back to the bedroom.

And then jumped out of my skin at the sound of feet pounding down the stairs above me. The front door of the upstairs apartment banged shut.

I raced to the window at the front of the house and looked out, but all I could see was the vague suggestion of a figure hurrying down the passageway opposite, so vague it might just have been my eyes trying to make something out of the shadows. Then the moon came out from behind a cloud and illuminated the empty street.

Whoever it was had disappeared.

I climbed back into my bed and looked at the clock: 3.20am. I rolled over, cursing as the crying started again upstairs, but this time it was quieter, more controlled, accompanied by a dull scraping noise, like someone dragging a chair across the floor. I let out the breath I'd been holding in, trying to relax, then tensed again at a sudden loud thud.

I waited for more, but all was finally silent.

I slept late the next day, not waking until 9am. Despite the fact that I haven't had a 9-5 job since my early twenties, I hate sleeping in; it feels like half the day's gone.

I got up and quickly showered and dressed. I decided I should probably ring Susie today, but she beat me to it -- the phone rang just as I finished eating breakfast.

"Hi S-"

"What The Actual Fuck is going on there?" I could hear the capital letters in her voice. She sounded - angry? upset? I wasn't entirely sure.

"Are you all right, Suze? I'm sensing a disturbance in the force..."

"I'll disturb your bloody force in a minute, Bella!" she cried.

Angry, then. "I've just been reading the world news on the BBC. When were you going to tell me there's a sodding serial killer on the loose in Venice?"

"Technically he's not a serial killer, you have to kill three or more people to –"

"Don't get smart with me, lady!" she said.

I smiled. "Sorry, Mum," I said. "Look, honestly, it's fine, I'm safe –"

"I know you're safe, but what are you doing about the murders? Are you writing about them? This is just the best thing that could've happened, isn't it? Two murders and you're on the spot! Well, now I know I can contact the local police and try to get you an 'in' –"

I smiled again, hoping I sounded as smug as I felt. "Ah now, Susie, I'm going to have to stop you there, because I already have the most spectacular 'in' on this one. I'm working with Interpol."

I could hear her sharp intake of breath; she was impressed. "Wow, that is absolutely bloody amazing! Are you shadowing them?"

"Better than that." I paused for a moment, all the better to enjoy it. "I'm working with one of their agents as a consultant."

"Oh my god, it gets better! What about your new man-friend? Does he mind you spending time with this hunky Interpol agent?"

"He *is* the hunky Interpol agent..."

Susie actually whistled; she was that impressed.

"Well I think I know who the main protagonists are going to be in your new book, then."

I laughed. "Oh how well you know me..."

Susie sighed, sounding much calmer now.

"Great! So now I know your writing's back on track, tell me - how's it going with the new man? Come on, I want the gossip!"

"There's still not that much to tell –" *apart from the fact that I am already crazy about the man even though I hardly know him.*

"Hasn't he succumbed to the famous Bella charm yet?" Susie sounded amused.

"What's famous about my charm? Apart from the fact it doesn't seem to work?" I asked.

"Oh dear. He does like you, though?"

I thought back to that first kiss...and the kiss goodbye, last night...and the way he gently reached over to touch on my hand while we were talking, and the fairy lights on the boat, and our picnic –

"Yes," I sighed. "He definitely likes me. He said he likes me so much that he wants to take it slowly and not muck things up."

"Awww, he sounds so sweet!" she said. "But frustrating. Maybe you need to be proactive. If I were you I'd jump him."

"Yes, I know you would," I said. "You are one scary mother when it comes to men."

"Guy likes it."

"Will wouldn't."

"Oh, it's Will is it? Will and Bella. Bella and Will –"

"What the happy fuck are you doing?"

"I'm just trying it out to see if you sound like a couple. You do."

"Goodbye, Susie..."

"No, wait! I –"

I put the phone down on her and smiled to myself.

"Bella and Will. Sounds good to me!"

I had a productive morning – more writing, no noise from above to disturb me – until 12pm, when there was a knock on the door. Will.

"Am I too early?" he said. "I couldn't wait any longer..."

I smiled, kissed him and grabbed my bag.

We walked through the streets until we reached the curve of the Grand Canal, then followed it to the Rialto Bridge, the reflections of its famous arches in the water below scattering whenever a boat or *vaparetto* passed under it. We joined the throng of tourists crossing over, window-shopping briefly as we passed the shops under those arches, full of jewellery, glass, masks and souvenir t-shirts.

We weaved our way through the food market, stalls with striped awnings laden with fresh fruit and vegetables, Will pointing out the now-empty fish market behind us; you had to get there early to buy fish, but the smell lingered forever.

"I know a story about the Rialto Bridge," I said. Will gave a big mock shudder.

"I hope it's not like the last one," he said. I laughed.

"Well, this time it's about the bridge builder. Oh, and the Devil..."

"Again? He gets in everywhere, doesn't he?" Will said.

"Yep. When they first started building the Rialto, the design caused them some problems. It was a very modern piece of engineering, and they kept getting half way across and the stone arch that forms the main span would fall apart and end up in the canal. That bit's historically true, by the way. Money was starting to run out and the chief engineer was worried he'd lose his job and his young family would be ruined."

We passed a row of gondolas, bobbing gently on the tide. The gondoliers sat in the shade, drinking and chatting as they waited for customers in the scorching sun. Watching the dazzling ripples on the water and listening to the buzz of the tourists, it seemed like the last place on earth that anything untoward could happen. I continued my story.

"In despair, the engineer prayed that someone would help him. And, as he so often does in these stories, the Devil appeared."

Will flung his hands in the air. "Ta da!"

I sniggered. "You make *such* a camp devil, but anyway... The Devil promised to help him, but in return he wanted the soul of the first living creature to cross the bridge. The engineer agreed."

Will sucked his teeth and shook his head. "Oh, I wouldn't do that if I were you..."

"They never learn, do they?" I laughed. "So the bridge was completed. The engineer, who between you and me was a bit of an arsehole, decided he would cheat the Devil by sending a chicken over the bridge."

Will burst into laughter, scaring the bejesus out of an old man who was napping in the sunshine on a chair outside his house. "What?!"

"Stay with me – he decided that on the morning of the opening ceremony, before all the bigwigs arrived, he'd send a chicken across first and the Devil could drag his poor little chickeny soul down to Hell. But – there's always a but – on the night before, while the engineer was in his office finalising his plans for the next day, the Devil appeared before his wife disguised as the engineer's assistant. He told the wife that her husband would be working late, and therefore she needed to take him his dinner. The wife, not knowing about the engineer's diabolical pact, agreed but as it was late she could not find a boatman to take her across the canal. The Devil had told her that the bridge was safe, so she went across that instead. The minute she reached her husband, the Devil appeared again and said, 'The bridge is built, I have kept my part of the deal; now you shall keep yours'. And he took the soul (and life, obviously) of the engineer's unborn son, along with that of his heavily pregnant wife."

"You really do have to watch the small print when you're dealing with workmen," said Will sagely, shaking his head. We laughed and kept walking.

"Where are we going?" I asked, getting jostled by the passing crowd. Will reached out and grabbed my hand to pull me back to him, then kept tight hold of it.

"There's this fantastic street food place on Calle dei Meloni," he said, enthusiastically. "They fry up prawns and squid and whatever fish they've landed each day until they're really crispy and serve them up in a paper cone, so you can walk about and eat at the same time. I love the food here but it's making me fat, so if I can eat and exercise at the same time..."

I laughed. "Sounds perfect!"

We reached the café and joined the queue at the counter in the window. Will had just ordered us two *fritto misto de mare* with polenta chips when his phone rang. I grabbed the two paper cones, the food inside hot and smelling delicious, as he answered.

"*Si?*" he looked over and caught me indelicately biting the tail off a prawn that was sticking out of the cone. He grinned, but then looked serious. *"Dove?"*

He listened intently, saying a few words in Italian that I, of course, didn't understand, then disconnected the call.

"It's a good job we chose a moveable feast for lunch," he said, grimly. "There's been another murder. Let's go."

CHAPTER SEVENTEEN

W e headed back towards the Grand Canal and took a water taxi downriver towards the Peggy Guggenheim Collection. We pulled over at San Vio just as the white stone walls and impressive landing stage of the museum came into view. Will paid the boatman and we jumped out onto a wooden jetty.

"Have you been to the museum yet?" he asked casually, for all the world as if we were just out for a stroll and not going to investigate another murder. "I must take you, it's really worth spending some time there..."

I followed him across Campo San Vio, into Calle della Chiesa and onto a small, ornate wrought iron bridge. A restaurant, Agostini's, stood on the other side, and members of what I assumed were the kitchen staff sat smoking on the steps of the bridge, looking pale and shaken.

"This place doesn't look much from the outside," said Will, "but it's one of the best restaurants in Venice. Really hard to get a table."

We weaved through the shocked kitchen staff outside and reached the front door. I wrinkled my nose.

"I don't think I'll be eating here in a hurry," I said. "It's smells like somebody burnt the main course."

"I don't think *anyone* will be eating here for a while," said Will, leading the way in.

Through the door, into the restaurant. More white-faced staff members sat at a table as two *polizia* interviewed them, their eyes flicking nervously towards another door at the back of the room. We walked past them, the sickly sweet smell of charred meat growing stronger.

"The restaurant only opens in the evening," said Will. "The staff had just come in to prep for the dinner service later on and that's when they found him."

Will reached out to push the door open. I tried not to breathe in too deeply – I had a horrible feeling I knew what was causing the smell and really didn't want to inhale any more than I had to.

The kitchen was small but well organised; the head chef obviously ran a tight ship. It would have been easy enough for the murderer to find a weapon – a sharp knife to fillet someone with or a heavy pan to swing at the victim's head. But they'd foregone all of that and turned to another bit of kitchen equipment that sat in the corner.

The victim was dressed in black robes. His hands were pinned to the kitchen counter with metal skewers, kebabed into place either side of an industrial-sized deep fat fryer that was currently occupied by his head.

I could feel the hysteria and the *fritto misto* I'd just eaten rising inside me. I swallowed hard.

"What's with the dress?" I asked. Will frowned.

"You mean the robes? He looks like a priest," he said.

"So he's a deep fat friar?"

Will looked at me. The hysteria and nausea were threatening to overwhelm me. I tried to hold it back; I was wearing my inappropriate sense of humour like a suit of armour and if I let even one chink appear in it I would totally lose my shit.

"Being fried would be bad enough," I said, beginning to wobble. "But drowning in hot fat? You'd be fighting to breathe and then your lungs would fill with burning oil and you'd start cooking from the inside –"

Will looked at me, white faced, and held out his hand to steady me. I pushed him away.

"I'm not going to faint," I said. "But I think I am going to –" And then I spewed.

I sat on the edge of the footpath, far away from the smell of over-cooked cleric, feet dangling into the cold waters of the Grand Canal. I struggled to get a grip on myself, but every time I felt calmer my mind wandered back to the image of the dying man, struggling to catch his breath and writhing in agony as the boiling hot fat filled his mouth, throat and lungs, smelling his own insides burning –

I dry heaved again and tried not to notice that the fish in the canal had started nibbling the remains of my lunch, floating on the water. So that was meat and fish off the menu for dinner tonight, then.

I shuffled along a bit further, not trusting my wobbly legs to carry me.

"There you are!" Will sat down next to me, looking at me in concern. "Feeling better?"

"Feeling empty," I said, and burped. "Oops. Sorry."

He took a stick of chewing gum from his pocket and handed it to me. "Here, I find it helps. And it'll make your mouth taste nicer."

I popped the minty gum into my mouth and chewed. It took away the taste of regurgitated fish and aroma of charred –

I steered myself away from that thought.

"Do you want to hear any more about the case?" Will asked gently. "I won't tell you if you don't feel up to it."

"No, I'm fine, honestly." I forced a smile and sat up straighter. "Hit me with it."

"Ok. Well, the victim *was* a priest – Father Antonio Pittaluga. He had his wallet on him. He was parish priest at a church in the Cannaregio sestieri and lived in the same area, so what he was doing over here after midnight is anyone's guess."

"Someone lured him over here," I said.

"We don't know that –" Will began.

"Yes we do!" I insisted. "Why else would he be here? Not on official church business. Not after midnight, in someone else's parish."

"Manera's trying to trace the owner of the restaurant to see if he can shed any light on why a priest would end up dead in his kitchen, but he apparently went on a hastily-arranged business trip out of the city."

"Who is the owner?" I asked.

"Pio Agostini," said Will. "You might have heard of him? He's a pretty successful restaurateur – he's got several restaurants in Rome and Florence, as well as this one. Does a lot of work for charity. He's well known and well loved in Venice."

"This won't be good for business though, will it?"

Will shook his head. "It won't be good for this particular restaurant, no. But it'll be water off a duck's back for Agostini. He'll shut this one down and concentrate on his businesses elsewhere, then in a year or two he'll open up again in another part of Venice. It won't stop him for long."

"And in the mean time, we still don't know how the priest ended up as dish of the day..." I shuddered again.

Will looked out across the canal. "The forensic team are there now. When they pulled the victim out they saw he had a deep head wound, and they think it was made by a marble rolling pin they found on the floor, under one of the cupboards. So he was probably dead or at least unconscious when he was stuck in the fryer."

I stared at him, fighting the sudden surge of hysteria rising again.

"You mean he was battered?" I gave a burst of insane laughter, which almost immediately turned into a massive crying fit.

Will hugged me tight and stroked my hair, trying to calm me down. The tears were just starting to subside when a thought occurred to me.

"The faceless priest..." I said. Will looked at me, quizzically.

"Will, it's another story!" I cried.

"What – like the doctor in the bell tower –"

I nodded. "And the mask maker and the Devil. Holy fuck..."

I took some deep breaths and tried to remember the story properly.

"There once was a priest, who was a good man. But he grew tired of hearing the seemingly pious people of his parish repent for their sins on a Sunday, only to spend the rest of the week living lives of greed and profligacy. He began to feel that the lessons he delivered from the pulpit fell only on deaf ears. Disillusioned and losing his faith, he started to steal from his own church and entertain lustful thoughts towards his female parishioners. One night, after Mass, he lured a beautiful young girl to a deserted place and defiled her."

Will stared at me, eyes wide as his listened.

"The priest was immediately struck with remorse and guilt. He ran to the church and prayed for forgiveness, but it didn't help; he thought that everyone would be able to see the sin he'd committed on his face. So he threw himself into the fire. God saw that he was truly repentant and saved his life, but the priest's face was burnt away."

I turned to Will.

"Don't you see? The evil doctor thrown from the bell tower. The mask maker killed by his own creation –"

"Well, his throat had actually been cut, but –"

"You can't deny the mask had a very special place in the murder, though," I said. "And now the faceless priest. What sin had he committed that needed burning away?"

Will looked grim. "What sin do we suspect the others of committing?"

"We don't suspect them, we know they did it!" I said, hotly. "And he's a priest. He wouldn't be the first one, would he?"

Will looked at me, troubled, then put his arm around me again. I leaned against him.

"There are twenty five stories in that book," I said, in a tone much calmer than I felt. "Three down, twenty two to go."

He hugged me tighter. "There are not going to be another twenty two murders, I promise you that," he said.

"You sure you'll have caught the killer by then?" I asked.

For a moment Will didn't answer. Then - "Nobody gets away with murder that many times."

We sat and watched the boats go by, the tourist hordes getting on and off gondolas and ferries and invading the Doges Palace across the water. Will kissed me on the cheek and smiled gently.

"Enjoying your holiday?" he said. I laughed shakily.

"I'll never fit all this on a postcard," I said.

"Maybe we should have a day off from sleuthing tomorrow," he suggested. "A day to just relax and forget about all this. What do you fancy doing?"

"I still haven't been over to the Lido yet," I said. "Can we take your boat and go over there for the day?"

CHAPTER EIGHTEEN

The rest of the day passed quietly enough. Will had to go back to the murder scene and then the police station, but I'd had quite enough excitement for one day so he found me a water taxi and sent me home.

I lay on the bed, feeling shaky and empty save for the low-level hysteria that was taking a while to subside completely. I reached for Francesca's book and looked up the priest's story, noticing for the first time that the murders had occurred in the same order as the stories were in the book; the evil doctor followed by the mask maker, who was in turn followed by the faceless priest.

With trembling hands I turned the page to find the next story: the False Witness. I read it, my stomach turning over again at the fate that befell the unfortunate (but ultimately guilty) man.

I put the book down and tried to sleep, but I was too afraid that I'd fall straight back into conversation with the late Dr

Gerbasi and his mask-impaled friend, only this time they'd be joined by the deep fried priest.

———————

I picked up the phone and thought about calling Susie, but instead found myself dialling a different number. A number I hadn't dialled for far too long.

It rang: once, twice, three times – *what a shame, not in* I thought to myself, ready to disconnect quickly, but then she answered.

"Hello?" she sounded puzzled. She didn't recognise my number. I took a deep breath.

"Hi, it's Bella." There was silence, and for a moment I thought she'd hung up. "You still there?"

"Yes," she said. "I was just surprised. It's been a while."

"Too long," I said.

"Yes."

Awkward silence. I squeezed my eyes shut to stop tears forming.

"So – how are you? How's Terry and the boys?"

"They're fine. We're fine. Are you ok, Bella?"

Please don't ask if I'm ok.

"Yes, of course I am! I'm in Venice."

"Ooh, very nice," she said. "You on holiday?"

"I'm here to write a book."

"You're writing again?" She sounded pleased. "Good."

"And I've met someone," I said.

"Not another writer?"

I smiled at the thought of Will, polar opposite of the bastard unfaithful ex-husband.

"No, not another writer. After Joel I figured that one narcissistic sociopath in the relationship is probably plenty."

She laughed. "You said it, sister."

There was another, slightly less awkward silence.

"Well I'd better go. I just wanted to -"

"Bella," she said suddenly. "Come and see us when you get back from Venice, yeah?"

Bloody tears, threatening my mascara...

"I will," I said. *Put the phone down before you cry.*

"Promise?"

"I promise. Love you, Meggy." The words were out of my mouth before I even knew it.

"Love you too."

I hung up and went to the bathroom to wash my face. *Stop crying, woman. Hold it together. Find something to take your mind off it.* I should be good at that. I'd been keeping my mind off it for a very long time now, but these murders were dragging it all back up.

I sat down and opened up the laptop, but my mind was too flighty to concentrate on writing. I flitted around on social media for a while, reading Susie's latest post, and a much more pleasant thought sprang into my mind.

Be proactive, Susie had said.

I opened a new internet tab and started Googling...

I went to bed early that night, feeling much happier. I'd had a sweet goodnight text from Will, who was still caught up in Interpol stuff, and I now had a plan for the next day.

My eyes closed the minute my head hit the pillow. I fell into a deep and thankfully dreamless sleep, and when the crying and scraping noise started again at 3.20am I barely noticed it. Then a loud bang woke me with such a sudden start that I wasn't sure if it was real or I'd dreamt it. I lay in the dark with my heart thudding in my chest, waiting for it to get back to normal, before drifting off again.

The trip over to the Lido island the next day was short and uneventful, Will standing proudly at the wheel of *La Sirena* and looking like an overgrown kid with a big boy's toy. If he smiled any more broadly I think his jaw may have dropped off. I watched him, aware that my own smile was probably just as wide.

The sun shone, there was a light breeze, and everything was perfect. We moored at one end of the island and jumped off the boat. I slipped off my shoes – I love the feel of sand and water between my toes - and we walked along the beach to the public sunbathing area. Will was just about to pay for two sun loungers when I stopped him.

"Let's walk further on and see what it's like up there, shall we?" I said, innocently.

"All the private beaches are up that way," he said. "You can walk on the beach, but you have to book the sun loungers in advance."

"Let's just have a look," I smiled, and quickly walked on so he had to follow.

We passed the private beach clubs, and carried on walking in the gentle shallows, the warm water lapping the shoreline. I took Will's hand and smiled.

We reached the Excelsior Hotel's private beach.

"This is –" began Will. I stopped him with a kiss.

"Oh look, those two loungers are free." Of course they were free, I'd booked them the night before on the hotel's website. "Let's sit there!" I dragged him over to the seats, Will looking around anxiously.

"We shouldn't –"

"Live dangerously," I said, signalling discreetly to the cabana boy who was lurking nearby, waiting for his cue. He approached with a couple of long, cool drinks on a tray and I grabbed both, passing one to Will. "*Grazie mille!* See, they don't mind..."

Will smiled at me suspiciously, but sat down and sipped at his drink.

"Put it on my bill," I whispered to the cabana boy, who smiled and walked away.

We spent the morning just talking about nothing in particular, swimming, sunbathing, and occasionally making out when there was no one else around (we both felt too grown up for big public displays of affection, but we enjoyed a good snog when no one was looking).

Lunch time approached. I heard Will's tummy rumble and laughed as mine did too. "Great minds think alike!" I said.

"There's a nice place –" Will started, but I grabbed his hand and pulled him to his feet.

"I know a place too! Come on."

He followed, bemused but willing.

We sat at the hotel pool bar and drank mocktails while we ate pizza and salad. We had the place more or less to ourselves, the only other guests being a large family group on the other side of the pool; *Nonna* and *Nonno*, mum, dad, two little girls. It was the old grandpa's birthday by the looks of it, and he was getting a little bit merry. We watched the children playing in the water. The whole scene was a thousand times removed from where we'd been yesterday.

"Look at those two!" said Will, smiling at the children splashing their grandfather. "Cheeky little monkeys."

I watched them, and my heart ached.

"Yes."

Will looked at me. "Are you ok?"

"Yes... They remind me of my sister and me when we were little," I said.

"I didn't know you had a sister," said Will.

"No. I don't see her much. She moved to Manchester a few years ago to be near our dad." I hoped I sounded casual but discouraging. No.

"But you're not from Manchester, are you?"

I laughed, exasperated. "What was it you said the other day, about people not being good at taking a hint?"

He laughed too. "Sorry. But I want to know all about you, too."

I could hardly argue with that. "My parents split up when I was seven and Megan was five. It was fine, I don't remember them arguing or anything, I think they just out-grew each other. They stayed friends. Dad lived nearby all the time we were little and we saw loads of him. It was all very civilised. He moved to Manchester for work years later after we'd both left home."

"So you had a nice childhood, in spite of the divorce?"

"Yes...yes, on the whole."

"On the whole?"

"I need another drink, don't you?" I waved at the waiter, and Will took the hint.

We carried on eating in comfortable silence, enjoying the sun on our shoulders and the sea breeze in our hair. I looked across at him, and he was more relaxed and happy than I'd seen him so far.

"How do you keep doing it?" I asked Will, suddenly. He'd just taken a mouthful of food and stopped mid-chew.

"Doing what?"

"Your job. Dealing with these bloody horrible cases. Doesn't it get to you?"

He swallowed. "Oh, that. Not really. I've seen a lot of death over the years..."

"The Army?"

"Yes. I did a couple of tours in Afghanistan."

"Did you lose friends out there?"

"No..." he said slowly. "I mean, of course I know people who got killed or injured, but not my close friends. We were lucky. The area we were based in – the people there were actually happy to see us. They hated the Taliban, and they didn't want them to come back. They tried, of course, and that was when..." His words trailed off.

"Did you – did you have to –"

"Kill people?" he said sharply. "Yes, I did. It's not a nice feeling, killing anyone. Even if they deserve it."

He sipped his drink and looked away, out at the ocean. I felt bad for mentioning it.

"Hey," I said softly. "Hey! Will, you were a soldier. You were there to protect people. You had to do it."

"Yes," he said. "Yes, I did."

We sat in silence for a moment.

"Anyway," I said finally. "That's not really what I meant. I meant cases like this – paedophiles – how do you carry on caring about who did it? Most people would probably say that they got what they deserved."

"What about you?" Will stared at me. "Is that what you think?"

I thought for a moment, trying to put my feelings into words. "I've always seen myself as quite a civilised person," I said. He smiled at that. "Oh, I know I write gruesome stories and say fuck more than a woman's supposed to – "

He laughed. "I had noticed that. I quite like it."

I laughed as well then. "Well, the civilised, non-sweary part of me thinks that murder is murder, regardless of who the victim is. No one has the right to appoint themselves judge, jury and executioner. The doctor, the mask maker and the priest should have been arrested and charged, and then banged up for a very long time."

I looked over at the pool as the children shrieked with laughter, and I felt my insides harden.

"But the other part of me – a big part of me – thinks that if they'd been arrested, they'd have got away with it. The doctor was old and doddery, he's truly sorry, we can't lock up an old man in his final days... the mask maker was obviously mentally ill, he needs help, not incarcerating, send him to a hospital and he'll be out again in five years. And the priest – well, that fucker would probably end up the next bloody Pope –"

"You don't think much of the Catholic Church, then?" said Will.

"I don't think much of any institution that is quick enough to tell its followers how to live but overlooks the actions of its own ministers."

"So you think...?"

"I think the bastards deserved to die."

We sat quietly, watching the family gather their belongings together. Mum and Dad wrapped the kids in towels and ushered them inside, while the grandparents slowly stood up and packed away their sun cream. The old man took his wife's hand and kissed it, and she laughed, reaching up to touch his face lovingly.

Will and I turned to each other and both spoke at the same time.

"I –" "So–"

We laughed.

"Go on," I said. "I was only trying to break the silence."

He laughed. "Yes, that was a bit of a mood killer, wasn't it? Sorry."

"I started it. I think."

"Don't argue," he smiled, taking my hand and raising it to his lips. I touched his cheek and we lost ourselves in each other's eyes for a moment. *Swoon.*

The waiter came over and started to clear the table and we parted, embarrassed at being caught acting like a couple of soppy teenagers.

"Oh, I looked into your friend Francesca," said Will. "She made it to Australia. The passport you found had been reported lost and cancelled, and she'd been issued another one. Worry over."

"Oh good," I said. "I don't think I could take another mystery –"

. . .

There suddenly came a shriek from the other side of the pool. We looked up to see the old woman, shouting and pointing at the pool. The old man was in the water.

"*Il mio marito!*" she cried.

Before I even grasped what was happening, Will leapt up and kicked off his shoes. He ran to the pool and dived in, the poolside barman not far behind him. He dragged the old man over to the side, keeping his head above the water.

A couple of waiters and the barman leaned down and pulled the old man out of the water. Will climbed out and checked his breathing, but apart from being wet and confused the elderly man was fine.

I wrapped my towel over Will's shoulders.

"Oh my god, you were amazing!" I said, proudly, as other guests and staff began to appear. *Yes, he's mine, I'm with the hero...!*

Will smiled. "All in the line of duty, ma'am," he said, in what was possibly the worst American accent I'd ever heard. I laughed.

The hotel manager came over to check if he was ok. Will shrugged.

"I'm fine, it was nothing," he said modestly.

"No it bloody wasn't!" I cried. "That was so hot..."

The hotel manager smiled as I turned to him.

"I think we'll go up to our room now and get these wet things off."

"If Sir wishes, we can have them cleaned and returned to you for the morning?" said the manager.

Will looked bewildered. "No, that's fine, they'll dry..."

He looked at me, all at sea. "We haven't got a room, have we?"

I felt my cheeks start to burn. "Aaah..."

Will came out of the bathroom clad in a hotel bathrobe. I took his wet clothes from him and hung them over a chair on the sun-drenched balcony, then stepped back inside.

"I still can't believe you booked a room," he said. I shrugged, feeling a bit daft.

"I just thought we might want to stay overnight," I said. "I did book an extra room, in case you wanted your own..."

He smiled and pulled me towards him.

"Of course I don't want a room of my own," he said, drawing me close.

"Thank god for that, because I didn't really book an extra one."

He laughed and leaned forward to touch my lips softly with his. Then we kissed, slowly, deeply, until we were both breathless. I gently tugged at the belt of the bathrobe and slid my hands inside, eager to feel his warmth. He tensed and drew in a sharp breath, then relaxed as I wrapped my arms around him and kissed him again.

His hands found the zip of my sundress and pulled, and I stood back for a second to wriggle out of it. I stood there in my new white lacy bra and knickers, thanking god I'd put on a matching set that morning. I hate my body – hate the big thighs, the flabby tummy, the stretch marks – but Will gazed at me as if I was the most beautiful creature he'd ever seen, and I suddenly felt like a goddess.

Then we were both naked and on the bed, kissing hungrily. We rolled over and he pinned me gently onto my back, kissing my lips, my cheek, my neck (I love my neck being kissed), down to my breasts, tracing a circle around my nipples with his tongue, and then further on, downwards...

There are many different types of sex. Sometimes it's a joyful romp, flinging each other around the bed, bending yourselves into unlikely positions (some of which work better than others), giggling as one of you inadvertently farts during oral sex. Other times all you both want is a good old fashioned knee-trembler, a short hard fuck to get each other off with the minimum of fuss.

Both of those came later.

But right now this was the most beautiful, intense lovemaking I'd ever experienced. I shuddered with pleasure underneath him as he gazed into my face, neither of us breaking eye contact for one moment, even as he tensed and gave one final deep thrust and cried out. Then we kissed again, slowly, tenderly, and he collapsed onto me, head buried into my shoulder. I felt on the verge of tears and had to give myself a stern talking to in order to stop them; but then he rolled over and pulled me in for a cuddle, and a couple escaped from my eyes anyway. *Bloody hell, Bella, what was that?* Amazing, that's what it was. I took a deep shuddery breath and snuggled into his chest.

CHAPTER NINETEEN

I woke the next morning still lying in Will's arms, despite the fact I never fall asleep in anyone's arms – too worried I'm going to dribble on them in my sleep, or do something that will make them suddenly realise I'm not the sex goddess I was pretending to be last night, but just a typical flabby, occasionally flatulent middle-aged woman.

The sun poured in through a chink in the curtains, highlighting the tip of his nose. He was awake but hadn't realised that I was too. I reached up and gently traced his profile with my finger, smiling as he turned to me.

"Good morning, gorgeous," I said, kissing him. He laughed.

"I was just about to say that to you!" he said.

We cuddled for a while, neither of us wanting to accept that it was morning and we had to get up. But eventually his phone rang, rudely interrupting our love-in.

"Another murder?" I asked as he disconnected the call, not

sure whether I wanted him to answer yes or no. But he shook his head.

"No, it was just one of the case officers saying forensics have come back with nothing," he said. "So far, we've got no fingerprints or DNA at any of the scenes."

"Nothing at all?" I said, surprised. "Isn't that unusual?"

"It is, rather. It's very difficult not to leave *something* behind. Either the Venetian police are really incompetent or our killer knows exactly what they're doing."

"Or killers," I said. "It struck me after the first one, how hard it would be for just one person to chain Gerbasi up. He was old and frail, but if he was still alive when they dragged him up the tower that would've been really difficult, with him struggling. Even if he was dead, he'd still have been quite a weight, especially with that chain round his neck. And then Carlevaro – stringing his arms out like that – that wouldn't have been easy."

"No," said Will thoughtfully. I shook myself.

"Anyway, I don't want to spoil our morning talking about them!" I said. "We'd better go and make sure your boat's still there..."

We had breakfast on the terrace then walked down the beach, hand in hand, back to Will's boat which thankfully was still there, bobbing gently on the tide. We sailed back to Will's mooring.

"What are you doing now?" he asked. I didn't have any plans – I just wanted to spend the day with him. "Let me take you to the Guggenheim," he said.

I sniffed. "Maybe we should go back to yours and change first," I said. "Your clothes smell like the hotel swimming pool."

He took my hand and we walked through the streets towards the Arsenele, a quiet neighbourhood only ten minutes from Piazza San Marco, but a whole world away from the tourist hustle and bustle.

Will's rented apartment was down a narrow side street. A wrought iron gate led into a shady court yard, with a couple of chairs, a table and an ancient gnarled olive tree in a massive terracotta pot. "My reading spot," said Will, smiling.

He opened the front door and stood back to let me into his ground floor apartment. It was quite masculine – modern décor and very tidy, which I thought betrayed his army background. He saw me giving the place the once over and smiled.

"Seen everything?"

I blushed. "I'm sorry, it's the writer in me. It means I'm a – what do you call it - a 'keen observer of human nature'."

"Where I come from, we just call that 'being nosey'."

I slapped him playfully and he laughed.

"I'll just go and throw some clean clothes on," he said. "I won't be a moment."

He left the room and I immediately had a proper nosey around – I mean, I 'observed the room more keenly' (*yeah right, nosey cow!*). I tried to work out what items had come with the apartment and what belonged to Will. The framed print of a gondolier serenading a woman at her window -- I really hoped that had come with the apartment; but the small amber-coloured Murano glass cat, perched on the lamp table next to the sofa – now that could be Will's. I knew he liked cats.

There was a bookcase on the far wall and I turned my

attention to that. I always think you can tell a lot about someone by what books they read. They were all in English, so I assumed that Will had brought them with him, or found them in the English language bookshop near the Rialto; he'd told me that he liked to read, and of course he had his spot in the garden outside.

Let me see... Stephen King (of course – never trust anyone who doesn't possess at least one Stephen King book), James Patterson (yes), Carlos Ruiz Zafon (oh yes!), Tess Gerritsen (I definitely approved of that one)....The books leaned drunkenly on the shelf, out of place amongst all this very strict neatness – it looked to me like he'd taken a few books away. *Probably porn or Mills and Boon and he moved them in case I came round* I thought to myself, giggling slightly.

I stopped and sat down, then frowned as I spotted another pile of books – probably the ones missing from the shelf – that had been shoved unceremoniously under a table in the corner, a tablecloth covering most of the pile. My interest was piqued; I had to sneak a peek.

They were my books.

Well, five of them, anyway. They were all well thumbed, obviously read more than once, and they all had a photo of the author – a photo of ME - at the back of the book.

"That's better," said Will, coming back into the room. "I don't smell of chlorine any –"

He stopped dead as I turned to him, holding the pile of books.

"Normally I'd be delighted to meet a fan," I said. "But –"

"Bella! It's not what you think." He looked stricken.

"I don't know what I think!" I said, slamming the books down on the coffee table. "But you obviously know this is me, or why would you hide them from me? How long have you known who I am?"

"Since you told me the story about finding the boy's body," he admitted, guiltily.

"But that was ages ago! All that time, you've known who I am – you've known all about me –" I couldn't believe what I was hearing. "Why didn't you say anything?"

"Well why didn't you?" he said, angrily. "You gave me a false name, you obviously didn't want me to know who you were! When I realised, I didn't know what to do. I didn't want to embarrass you by calling your bluff. And I didn't think it really mattered at that point. I didn't know that we'd – that this would happen – us –"

"It just feels really weird and stalker-ish," I said.

"That's not fair."

"Yeah, well," I said, sitting on the sofa and avoiding his eyes. I knew it wasn't fair, but I was freaked out. I also felt bad that in all our time together, as we got closer and closer, it hadn't occurred to me that I'd been lying to him; I hadn't even thought about the fact that I'd started our relationship by pretending to be someone else.

Will reached out and picked a book off the pile: my debut novel, *The Boy on the Beach* (yeah, I know, not a great title but to be fair it did what it said on the tin).

"You write like you talk, did you know that?" he said, carefully.

I shrugged. "It's called your 'writer's voice'," I said. I didn't like my voice the way it came out then, but I couldn't help it.

"I know. But in your case, it really is your voice. Reading your books – it always felt like I was having a chat with you." Will sat next to me, but I still wouldn't look at him.

"If that's supposed to make this feel less creepy, it ain't working," I said.

He sighed. "I don't mean it felt like you were talking only to me, just that – oh god, I don't know. I suppose I thought you sounded like you'd be a nice person to talk to."

I opened my mouth to make another sarcastic comment but he stopped me. "And yes, I know that sounds just as pathetic and obsessive and weird, but it's not meant to be. I thought it in the same way that I think Stephen King would probably be great to sit around the fire with, swapping spooky stories and drinking beer."

"He is," I said, absentmindedly. Will's eyes widened.

"Wow. Well, there you go. Look, I understand why you lied to me when we met – I understand that people have probably treated you differently when they've found out who you are, that you're rich and famous. But you have to understand how it was – is –for me."

He flicked through the pages of the book.

"This book – this book really helped me, you know. When it came out I was in a very bad place. A friend of mine told me I had to read it. When I saw what it was about – I didn't really want to. But he insisted I should, so I did." He sighed. "I started it 8 o'clock at night and I'd finished by 4 am."

He put the book down and turned to me.

"I read an interview with you about it – where you told the story about finding the boy's body. The interviewer asked if you'd had any experience of abuse in your own life. " I shifted uncomfortably in my seat. "And I was amazed when you said no, because in the book – it's just like you could see into the little boy's head."

He swallowed hard and I looked at him, and I knew in that gut wrenching moment exactly what he was going to say next.

"Like you could see into *my* head."

"Oh Will..." I reached out to touch him but he shrugged me off.

"It started when I was 11," he said. "I tried to stop him. For years I thought it was my fault, that I must've done something to make him do those things to me."

"Of course it wasn't your fault!" I cried.

"I know that now. But I didn't realise it until I read your book. So if you think this is weird for you, just think how it feels to me, to have this amazing person, this person who helped me through a really bad time in my life without even knowing it, to have her sitting next to me right now, sharing my bed –" He stopped, overcome.

I grabbed him and pulled him to me, as he sobbed into my shoulder.

"I'm so sorry Bella," he wept, his body shuddering. "I didn't mean to fall in love with you –"

"I love you," I said, hugging him fiercely and stroking his hair. I could feel my own tears coming and sniffed furiously, trying to be the strong one. I've always been the strong one. "I'm sorry, Will. I should have trusted you. No more secrets, ok?" He wept harder against me, while I ignored the voice at the back of my head that sneered back at me, *no more secrets.*

We sat there for about an hour, hugging and crying and whispering soothing things to each other. And then we went to bed and stayed there.

CHAPTER TWENTY

Will and I spent the whole of that day in his apartment, in our own little world safe from reality. We made love, and talked, and sat in the garden eating *arancini* brought round by his neighbour (a lovely warm Italian mamma, who lived with her grown up son and obviously felt responsible for the lonely *inglese* who rented her ground floor rooms).

Then we made love again. I was beginning to find it difficult to walk... I understood now why Will had been concerned about rushing into a relationship with me. He'd tried so hard to make his marriage work, but in their four years together he'd never told his ex-wife about his past, and when she started talking about having a family he'd freaked out; he'd heard too many theories about victims of abuse becoming abusers themselves, and despite never having had the slightest urge to touch a child, he was terrified of becoming what he most despised. Sex itself was something he'd used quite freely in the past to make himself feel better, but it also came with bad memories attached, and (he told me) he'd always found it difficult to equate the sweaty, grunting, thrusting act of having sex with showing someone that you loved them. He'd been celibate for three years by the time we'd met, and felt that it had helped him quiet his inner demons (his words, not mine).

Whatever, I was overwhelmed that he was able to trust me enough to let me in. I'd fallen for him in a huge way, and it seemed he felt the same for me. I was happier than I had been for a long time.

We went to bed and both fell into an exhausted sleep, worn out not just by our physical exertions (of which there'd been many) but by our emotions too.

I was so tired but so happy that I didn't expect to see Gerbasi in my dreams.

He was waiting for me propped up on the rusting bed frame again. He looked very uncomfortable and, although he raised a hand in greeting, he didn't turn his head towards me.

"What's the matter with you?" I asked. I was really starting to get pissed off with him.

He turned his body towards me but his head stayed where it was, jammed in against the bed frame. I could see the raw, ragged meat of his neck where the chain had cut through it. Gerbasi raised his hand again, waving it around expressively as a thin watery gurgle emanated from his exposed windpipe.

"I don't understand –" I said.

He turned his body back so it lined up with his head and tried again, this time the words coming out of his mouth but with a strange, airy quality to them, as if the breath was escaping through the slit in his neck as he spoke.

"My head's come off," he said. I rolled my eyes.

"Yes, I can see that!" I snapped. "Where's your friend?"

He raised his hand and pointed to the other side of the courtyard, where Father Pittaluga was attempting to remove the carnival mask from Carlevaro's arse.

"He'll never manage it." Gerbasi sounded amused. "That mask is wedged there for all eternity. Or at least until his sphincter muscle rots away and it falls out."

We watched the two hapless corpses in companionable silence for a moment. Pittaluga reached for the mask but he couldn't grasp it; maybe because the two metal skewers in his hands hampered him, but mostly because his eyes had been fried in their sockets and he couldn't see.

"Left a bit – left-" Carlevaro tried to direct him but the priest couldn't tell his left from his right.

"Imbeciles," said Gerbasi.

"Twats," I agreed. "So, anyway, this has been very entertaining and all, but is there a point to me being here? You know I'm not going to avenge your death."

"No, but you still want to know who did it, don't you?" He smiled smugly, and for a moment I hated him because he was right. But then I remembered that his head had come off, and I felt better.

"So are you going to tell me, then?" I asked. "Because the police haven't found anything."

"Call me an old cynic," he said. "But I don't think they've been looking that hard, do you?"

"Well..." I thought about it. Manera and his men had been quite laid back about the investigation, but then this was Venice, not London or New York. *La Serenissima* was, well, pretty serene and calm generally, the Venetians not ones to make an undue fuss, and as a result they weren't exactly set up to handle this sort of crime.

"They don't want to make a big scene over the likes of you," I said. "They wouldn't want to alarm the tourists, would they?"

"Balls," said Gerbasi. I was slightly shocked.

"Well instead of being a whiny bitch about it and talking in enigmatic riddles, why don't you just tell me?"

Gerbasi shook his head in disgust. "I'm dead and you still expect me to do all the work for you," he said. "No rest for the wicked. But ok. Read the book she left you."

"Read the book?"

He nodded – or tried to. His head didn't move.

"Drat!" he said. "Yes, read the book. It's the whole reason you're here."

I looked at him thoughtfully, then started as above us the bell tower began to chime. I looked up, dreading who I was going to see swinging there tonight.

It was my elderly neighbour.

I woke up with a jump, making Will murmur in his sleep and roll over. I kissed the back of his neck and rolled the other way, looking at the bedside clock before I closed my eyes.

3.20am...

The next day I rose early, smiling at Will still sleeping with an expression of pure peace on his face. *God I love that man* I thought, and felt a warm thrill run through me.

Life was looking up. My book was coming along so quickly it was almost writing itself, and I could see myself spending the rest of my days with this sweet, funny but complex man I'd run into at random at a café. Funny how things work out.

I made tea and brought Will a cup, sitting next to him on the bed as he woke up.

"Good morning, sleepyhead!" I said, kissing him lightly on the top of his head.

He saw that I was already dressed and frowned. "Why are you up so early?" he asked. "And why have you got clothes on?"

I shrieked as he grabbed me and pulled me to him for a kiss. I sat up again.

"As much as I wish I could spend my entire life in bed with you, I have to finish my book. I have work to do," I said. "And so do you!"

He groaned.

"Drink your tea and get up! Interpol aren't paying you to lie around in bed and pleasure your new girlfriend," I said, sternly. "Oh, such pleasure..."

He laughed. "So – that was all right, then? Last night?"

"Last night, and yesterday afternoon, and the day and night before that –"

He sat up and held my face in his hands, then kissed me tenderly. I'm normally like *yuck, morning breath* but I didn't care. I may even have swooned momentarily.

"Oh you're making this very hard for me," I murmured. He grabbed my hand and lowered it.

"And you're making this very hard for me," he said, kissing me again.

No! I had to be strong. I danced out of his grip and grinned at him.

"Hold that!" I said. "That thought, not your...."

He laughed. "Ok. And I'll hold you to that. Not the thought but my... "

"Steady now!" I giggled. I bent down to kiss him one last time and headed out of the room.

"Bella?" he called. I stuck my head round the door.

"Yes?"

"Type quickly."

I danced out into the street and somehow made my way back to Francesca's apartment, floating along the canals and passageways feeling as light as a feather.

When I reached the front door I looked up at the neighbour's window, the scene from last night's dream - her elderly body twisting and kicking and twitching in the air – briefly crossing my mind. I was surprised to see that the light was on. But it was still reasonably early, and I knew that the old lady was often up late (and never worried about keeping me awake, too).

Inside, I had a long, luxurious shower, enjoying the feel of the hot water on my skin. The last two days and nights had taken their toll on my body, and I was aching in areas I hadn't ached in for quite some time, but I didn't care. I stood under the gently pummelling spray for as long as I could stand the smell in the bathroom – those famous Venetian drains seemed to be playing up today.

Dressed, reinvigorated and with a cup of tea in hand (essential writer kit), I flipped open the laptop and sat at the desk, gazing out of the window.

Then I started to write. My protagonists had found a body in the bell tower, one in the mask shop and one in a nearby restaurant. I had the perfect ingredients for a murder mystery, with a side order of love thrown in. I sighed. Now to wrangle it into a satisfying ending...

I worked for an hour, then stopped for a breather. I checked my emails and finally, there was one from Charlie McArthur, ex-crime writer and public school English teacher.

Hi Bella,

Lovely to hear from you! Apologies for the long delay in replying – it's the school holidays here, I've been away and not been checking my emails very often!!

I came back to school last week to prepare for the new term, so I've had a few days to look into the incident you mentioned. There's not really anything on record here – it's a little vague – but I can tell you that the dates you gave me for the doctor teaching here are a bit out. He left in 1983, not 85, and then went to teach at St Barnabas School in Oxfordshire. He didn't get to the other school you mentioned, Woodford House, until May 1985.

The rest of the email went on about his work and other things that, to be honest, I wasn't that interested in, although I was glad to hear that he was still writing (romance novels under a female pen name). St Barnabas School...I looked at the list Will had given me, but it definitely wasn't on there.

I searched for the school on the internet and soon found its website. It was a beautiful old school, with a good reputation... I worked my way through the pages, nodding sagely to myself at the fact there was no mention of how much it cost to send your son there (which meant it was ridiculously expensive); looked at the photographs of the grounds, the facilities, the bright happy faces of the students... I wasn't sure what I was looking for, but I doubted there'd be a page listing all the paedophiles they'd had on the staff over the years.

I clicked on the tab marked 'History' and started to read about the school's founders; then onto more recent history – pictures of the boys from back in the 1950s – winning cricket and rugby teams...

I was stopped for a moment by the smell. It was quite pungent now. The drains really were playing up. I stood and opened the doors onto the balcony, stepping out to get a breath of fresh air, and then I heard it; the crying from upstairs. I sighed; the peace and quiet of the last couple of days had been too good to last. Maybe I should have felt more sympathetic towards the old dear, but really it was starting to piss me off. I shook my head and went back inside.

I sat down and touched the finger pad to wake the screen up again...and then gasped in shock.

It was a picture of the victorious 1983 Under-14s cricket team. They sat in rows on a couple of benches in the time honoured team photo set-up, coach or sports teacher standing next to them, captain in the middle, shield or trophy or whatever at his feet.

Two boys away from the captain, smiling that slightly shy smile I'd come to love, was Will.

There was a list of names along the bottom of the picture: *Wilson B, Stuart J, Carmichael W...*

I felt the room spin for a second and held tightly onto the desk until it had passed.

Will had been sexually abused as a boy.

He'd gone to St Barnabas school.

Where Dr Santino Gerbasi had taught Latin.

CHAPTER TWENTY-ONE

I was roused from my shock by a scream from upstairs. I jumped up from the desk and stood, listening; that had sounded like a proper, terror-filled scream, not just the incessant bloody crying I was getting used to from my neighbour.

And then I heard that horrible voice again; low and gravelly, as if spoken through a mouth full of graveyard soil: "*Ci vediamo all'inferno, puttana!*"

And the scraping noise, like a chair being dragged heavily across a wooden floor. A pause, then a loud bang, then silence.

Heart pounding, I walked slowly across to the front door, listening for – praying for – sounds of movement, of life upstairs, something to tell me that the old lady was ok and that I didn't need to go and knock on her door again. But there was nothing.

I went outside and stood in front of her door, hand raised, taking a deep breath...

And then the door flew open violently, making me yelp. There was no one behind it. But the smell...oh god, the smell...it was a smell I'd been getting used to over the last few days. The smell that had pervaded the island of Poveglia, Carlevaro's mask shop, and even the restaurant where Pittaluga had met his hideous end, lurking under the aroma of burnt flesh.

And I could hear buzzing.

"Hello?" I called up the stairs in a weak voice. I didn't expect a reply, and I didn't get one.

I slowly stepped over the threshold and put my foot on the first stair. I shook my head at my own nervousness – *"the dead can not hurt the living,"* Gino had said – and walked up the stairs, my breathing getting heavier and louder in my ears.

Dr Santino Gerbasi stood in front of me, head still on – just – but white, bloodless, with the chain around his neck. I whimpered and my bladder gave up. *But I'm not asleep* I whispered to myself. The late doctor wasn't looking at me though.

He was looking at the twisting, turning body of my elderly neighbour, which hung from a wooden beam by a length of what looked like sheets, knotted together into a rope.

"Ci vediamo all'inferno, puttana!" Gerbasi snarled at the poor woman, who kicked and twitched in terror. And then she stopped. Gerbasi turned to me and I backed away, towards the window overlooking the canal.

"No – please..." I pleaded. With a snarl, the doctor reached towards me – and then disappeared into thin air. I whimpered, back pressed against the window frame.

The hanging corpse turned to me. I could feel myself on the verge of just giving up, passing out and letting whatever was going to happen, happen, but I forced myself to stay upright.

The elderly neighbour stepped down from her noose and smiled at me.

"Finire la mia storia," she said, reaching out her hands to me. *"Finire la mia storia!"*

Then she floated into the air and flew at me in a rush of wind that blew open the shutters and the window, knocking me off my feet.

I struggled upright again and looked around but the ghosts of the old lady and the doctor had disappeared, leaving me alone with the slowly swinging, flyblown corpse.

I ran to the window and screamed. "Please help me! Help!"

The police came, and the ambulance boat, but the old lady had been dead for some time. The police officer – not one I'd seen before at a crime scene – asked me in perfect English when I'd last seen or heard the deceased. I decided it was best not to tell him that I'd seen her just now and she'd left me a message, or that I'd been hearing her at the same time every night for the last week, despite the fact she must have been dead already.

The last time I was certain that she'd been alive was when she'd had the argument with the quiet man who may or may not have disappeared into the mist when I looked out of the window. I didn't mention him, either; it was clear that the unhappy woman had killed herself after he'd left. She'd dragged a wooden chair over to the beam – the scraping noise I'd heard – and then, once she had her head through the improvised noose, had kicked the chair away with a loud bang.

"How long had you known her?" the policeman asked.

"Oh, I didn't know her at all –" I began. He frowned.

"But she has emails from you on her computer," he said.

CHAPTER TWENTY-TWO

I made my way on shaky legs to Will's apartment. I knew in my heart that what I suspected was true, but I needed to hear it from him. And I knew that by confronting him I was putting myself in danger, but you know what? At that point, I didn't care. It wasn't just the rug that had been pulled from under me; it felt like the ground had.

I found him sitting in the courtyard, reading in the early evening sunshine without a care. He jumped up and rushed to open the wrought iron gate to let me in.

"At last!" he said. "You've been gone all day. I was starting to get worried."

He leant in to kiss me; I let him.

"Is something wrong?" he asked, worried.

"Can we go inside?"

We went indoors, Will glancing over at me, seriously concerned now.

"What's happened?" he said, shutting the door behind him.

"The old lady upstairs killed herself," I said. "I found her."

A whole raft of expressions – fear, guilt, even a touch of relief, I thought – crossed his face before he reached out to take my hands.

"Oh no, Bella! That's terrible," he said. I pulled my hands away.

"I'd never really spoken to her," I said. "But that's how she wanted it, isn't it? So I wouldn't work it out."

The fear on his face now was unmistakeable.

"Bella –"

"It explains why she always had that bloody stupid hat on as well, doesn't it? And the big glasses. In case I recognised her from the photo in her book. She made herself look years older, just by stooping and acting all doddery whenever she saw me. Can't believe I didn't see through it."

Will sat down heavily, not looking at me.

"When they told me it was Francesca hanging from the beam there, I was certain they'd made a mistake. Because you told me she was in Australia, didn't you? You checked. And you wouldn't lie to me, would you?"

Will started to cry. I was suddenly furious.

"Oh just quit the fucking crying!" I shouted at him. "I know you killed Gerbasi –"

"What?" he gasped.

"He was a fucking teacher at your school!" I said. "You told me you were abused as a child, and who was the bloody Latin teacher at your school? Gerbasi. Why did you kill the others? To throw Manero off the scent? But why Francesca?"

"I didn't kill her!" Will leapt up and grabbed me by the shoulders. "I didn't kill her or Gerbasi –"

I shook my head and tried to pull away, but he kept tight hold of me.

"Please, Bella, you have to believe me –"

"Why?" I sneered at him. "Because you've always told me the truth in the past?"

He let go and stood in front of me, arms hanging limply by his side. He looked defeated. And suddenly that's how I felt too. I didn't want to be right. I wanted him to take me in his arms and tell me that I'd got it all wrong. I wanted to believe him. And then I wanted to jump in his boat and sail away with him, somewhere far from bell towers and abandoned islands, mask shops and canal-side restaurants.

That's what I wanted, more than anything.

"Are you going to the police?" he asked. I looked at him for a moment and felt my heart break a little bit more.

"Tell me why I shouldn't," I said. "And tell me where I come into all this."

He'd been seconded to Venice as part of an on-going Interpol investigation into the Mafia (he said). All that he'd told me about that – with the son of the Mafia family leaving Sicily to set up a cheese shop in Venice – was absolutely true.

"It was great," said Will. "I'd already spent time in Sicily, so I knew the family and the way they operated, and I knew that for the moment the best thing to do was just keep an eye on him while he set up his business. All I really had to do was occasionally pop in and buy cheese. I spent most of my time getting to know the city, sight seeing, eating... I bought a boat! I've been thinking about retiring in a couple of years and it just felt like I was starting early.

And then I saw her..."

I looked up from the floor to see him staring into the distance, a stricken look on his face as he remembered.

"Francesca?"

He nodded.

"I hadn't seen her for thirty years, but she hadn't changed. She was still a striking woman. She was walking around the Rialto market, chatting to stall holders, laughing, flirting with them. And all I could do was stare at her and think how much I hated her."

He got up and poured himself a glass of wine, offering one to me too. After a moment's hesitation, I took it. We both downed them quickly and he poured more.

"I followed her home through the streets. I didn't think she knew I was there, but when I got to her apartment – the one you've been staying at, not the one upstairs – I found her sitting in the living room with the front door open, waiting for me. She thought I was there to kill her."

"And were you?"

"I don't know! I didn't know what to do. I'd pushed it all away, hidden it for so long, I had it all under control, and then I saw her and I was thirteen again and – "

He stopped, putting down the wine glass; his hand shaking. Despite what he'd done I felt some sympathy for him.

"What happened when you were thirteen?" I asked. "How was Francesca involved?"

I pictured it in my head as Will spoke. He'd been happy at St Barnabas on the whole – missed his mother at first, like all the boys did, but he soon made friends and settled in. He was doing well at his lessons, he was in the school cricket team (as I'd found out), and he and his best friend Daniel had discovered a way to sneak in and out of the grounds at the weekends so they could go to the cinema in the local town.

The new house mistress who had just started was pretty and still very young – not much older than the boys in the sixth form, who all had varying degrees of crushes on her. The fact that she was Italian made her all the more attractive.

Not so attractive, however, was the fact that the exotically-named Signora Gerbasi had also brought her brother to the school. Dr Gerbasi was a big, stout man with a broad smile and booming laugh that hid an unpleasant, bullying nature. He was there to teach the boys Latin, but he always found an excuse to come along and watch them play rugby and cricket, often helping out with the smaller children in the changing rooms afterwards. The bigger boys made jokes about him being queer, but no one really thought they were serious; besides, Will knew a couple of his friends liked other boys That Way, and they weren't perverts or anything, they just tended to be the ones who got the main roles in the school's annual theatre production.

I smiled at that.

One Saturday evening, when the boys were supposed to be in their form rooms, Signora Gerbasi found Will and Daniel sneaking back into the school after a clandestine afternoon at the movies. Rather than taking them to the head master, who would no doubt have administered the worst possible punishment – a letter home – she offered instead to take them to her brother; they wouldn't get off scot-free, but this way no one else had to know about it.

That evening was the beginning of two years of hell for Will and Daniel, and various other small, pretty boys who somehow found themselves on the Gerbasis' radar. Will wouldn't tell me what this 'punishment' was, but he didn't need to; it was clear from the look on his face.

Francesca, who seemed to live both in awe and terror of her older brother, would make sure the boys kept their appointments and deliver new miscreants to him. And Gerbasi – the big, stout man whose physicality brooked no refusal – punished and rewarded his boys in return, although Will could never tell what the difference between the two was.

"Why didn't you tell someone?" I asked, horrified at his story; but I knew why. Will, white-faced, shook his head.

"How could we?" he said. "We were just children. He was a teacher. You're supposed to do what the teacher tells you. He said that if we told anyone we'd get expelled, because then everyone would find out how bad we were. He was actually saving us from getting expelled by administering our punishment in secret."

I shook my head sadly and Will carried on.

As the abuse intensified, Will found ways of shutting himself off from it, of withdrawing into his head and waiting for it to be over. But Daniel – small, skinny, sensitive Daniel – couldn't. He became increasingly depressed. Will would often hear him crying in bed at night, and he would creep over to slide in next to him, comforting his friend in the only way he knew how.

Will swiped at his eyes. "I was only trying to show him that I loved him and I wanted to make him feel better, but I was just as bad as Gerbasi –"

"No you weren't!" I cried, reaching out to him then thinking better of it. "There's a world of difference between two friends the same age trying to give each other a little bit of comfort and what that bastard did."

"I was so confused, for years afterwards," said Will. "When I was in the Army I'd basically shag anything that moved, trying to make myself feel better. It never worked. I didn't know if I was gay, or just a pervert –"

"You're none of those things," I said softly.

He smiled sadly at me. "No. It took meeting you to make me realise that."

One day Daniel didn't come down for breakfast – he'd been loitering in the bathroom as the other boys got dressed, saying he was unwell. Will volunteered to go and check on him.

And found him hanging from the ceiling light in their dormitory.

After that, all hell broke loose. The abuse came to light, and the Gerbasi siblings were shown the door. But despite the death of one of their students, the police were kept out of it. The grief-stricken parents didn't want their son's memory tarnished, and didn't want to even think about what had driven him to take his own life; while the headmaster felt that it wouldn't be fair on the students – those who'd been victims as well as those who hadn't – to have the school under the spotlight. It was thought that it would be too stressful for the boys to have to go through the ordeal of making statements, or maybe even having to testify at a trial.

Will had begged his parents to report it, but they didn't really want to think about what had happened. And anyway, it was over now; the abusers had gone, and their son seemed fine. They talked about it once, then it was thought best that Will just forgot about it.

"Because it's that easy," I said, furiously.

Will looked at me. "You have to understand what it was like in my family. It wasn't that my parents didn't care. They were horrified – they just didn't know how to process it. God, we didn't even talk about sex until I was 21, and even then it was the most embarrassing conversation I think my father had ever had, especially when he realised there wasn't anything he could tell me that I didn't already know. My mother's idea of making things better was to take me out and buy me ice cream and all the toys I wanted, anything to keep me occupied. And my father's was to smile bracingly and trot out some platitude like 'worse things happen at sea' and 'what doesn't kill us makes us stronger'. I wish it *had* killed me."

"Don't say that!" I said, quickly.

"So you do still care about me, then?" he asked. I ignored the question.

"So – you're in Francesca's apartment thirty years later, deciding whether or not to kill her..." I said.

"I asked her why she did it. Why she stood by – why she helped that monster hurt us! I asked her if she ever thought about us. If she ever thought about Daniel. I was so angry, I leapt up and raised my hand to hit her –" Will trembled with the memory – "- and then she said my name."

"She remembered you?"

"She said she remembered all of us. Every. Single. One. She said she'd been waiting for the day when her sins would catch up with her, when one of her boys would hunt her down and kill her."

"So did you hit her?"

"No."

"Shame."

Will turned to me, his eyes blazing. "It's so easy for you to sit there and make funny remarks, isn't it? So easy to judge someone when it hasn't happened to you –"

My heart leapt, but of course he had no idea. "She helped her brother molest little boys –"

"Because she'd been molested too!" he cried. "It was all she knew. Her father used to touch her when she was a little girl. He told her that that was how you show someone you love them." He shifted uncomfortably. "But then he started to get too rough with her and she'd cry, and he'd put his hand over her mouth and tell her not to be a baby."

I swallowed hard, feeling sick, but I was still furious with the dead woman.

"Then she should've bloody known how you all felt –"

"He raped her for the last time when she was 14. It was his parting gift to her – she was getting too old for him. She had a child."

I looked at him in horror, feeling really sick now.

"A son. She loved him more than anything else in the world, but at the same time she couldn't bear to look at him because of who his father was. She had him adopted."

"Oh my god..."

"Getting pregnant at that age, in a strict Catholic country – it was the worst thing that could happen to a girl. She tried to tell her mother who the father was, but she wouldn't believe her. They kicked her out. The only one who believed her was her big brother Santino. He came to her rescue and took her in, looked after her while she was pregnant. He even offered to help her raise the child, but there was something about the way he offered that made her uneasy –"

"So she gave him up."

"What other choice did she have? Gerbasi said that no man would ever love her after what she'd done, but he did because she

was his sister. So he carried on looking after her, and in return she
–"

"In return she procured little boys for him!"

"She had to! She was a victim too. Don't you see? All that time I'd hated her, when I should've pitied her."

I smiled at him.

"You're a better person than me, then. To pity her –"

"Yes, I pitied her. Because even if they hadn't been found out, I'd have left the school in a few years. He would've stopped being my teacher. But that man would never stop being her brother."

After the tragedy at St Barnabas School, Francesca had attempted to escape her brother's clutches, moving from England back to Italy. She moved from village to village, never able to settle for fear that he would track her down. And he always did. Every time she thought she'd lost him, a postcard or letter would arrive from whatever school he was teaching at now. Just to let her know he hadn't forgotten her...

Finally, she found herself a protector: a kindly Italian writer, a gentle man who couldn't be more different to Gerbasi. They married. At last Francesca felt free of her brother, but not of her past -- she longed to see the child she'd had adopted.

She was able to trace him through the adoption agency. She didn't have the courage to approach him, but it was enough to know that he had a happy, loving family and was doing well at school and later, in his chosen career.

Francesca thought she had put the horrors of her life behind her, but every now and then they would re-surface in terrible nightmares. Her husband suggested she write those nightmares down; once on paper, maybe they would lose their hold over her.

She slowly began to channel those bad dreams into a book of

ghost stories – the same book that had lured me to Italy. She didn't intend to publish the book; it was more like therapy. The memories of her guilty past still lingered, but the love of her husband and her pride in the son she'd given up helped keep them at bay.

And then her husband became gravely ill. She nursed him for months, but to no avail. Her beloved protector died, and she was alone again.

Grieving but fearful that her brother would draw her back into his web again now that she was on her own, she moved to Venice to be near her son, and finally – after so many years – she found the courage to write to him. She was overjoyed when he responded with relative warmth; he was shocked, but he'd always known he was adopted and he relished the opportunity to find out why.

She refused to tell him the whole truth, saying only that she'd been abandoned by his father, who was an uncaring man; but he accepted it and they formed a tentative relationship.

Francesca relaxed and began to enjoy life again. She loved Venice, loved the hustle and bustle of tourists which made it so easy to disappear, just a face in the crowd; loved the dark, winding canals and narrow streets that seemed to echo the dark and winding ghost stories that she was still writing. She finished her book, taking the plunge and publishing it, and had some small success.

But that success came with a price. Gerbasi tracked her down and, now retired and with no ties to any particular place, moved to Venice too. He still possessed the same tastes and desires – pretty young boys – but without his boarding school pupils, who'd always provided a rich seam of talent to pluck his next victim from, he had to work a little harder. He began to volunteer as a literacy teacher at a local charity for disadvantaged young boys, financed by the successful (and still currently missing) restaurateur, Pio Agostini. The spiritual health of the boys was handled by Father Antonio Pittaluga, who took them once a week for Mass, while a local mask maker, Roberto Carlevaro, ran arts and crafts workshops for them in the back room of his mask shop.

It was the beginning of the end for Francesca. In desperation she told her son the truth about his biological family. He was horrified. They argued. Francesca was alone again.

And then Will turned up on her doorstep.

CHAPTER TWENTY-THREE

W e'd finished the bottle of wine by this point and I was struggling to control my emotions. I'd even started to pity Francesca, despite her part in Will's suffering; but then I reminded myself that three men, despicable though they were, had been murdered. And murdered so theatrically, their corpses displayed in horrific tableaux to fit in with Francesca's ghost stories. Why?

And how had I ended up being a part of it all? I hadn't committed any crime here, but Will had asked me to help with the investigation. In my eagerness to get close to both him and the murders – the scent of a new book in my nostrils – I hadn't really thought about the fact that it was an unusual thing for an Interpol agent to do. I mean, in movies Interpol or MI6 or CIA agents are always getting civilians involved, using their psychic powers or hacking skills or whatever; but in real life? Really?

"Ok," I said, carefully, trying to marshal my thoughts.

"Gerbasi was a total bastard and so were his friends. I completely understand that you'd want them punished –"

"I didn't want them punished," said Will, angrily. "I wanted them to face justice – proper justice. You said it yourself, if they'd been arrested they would've escaped with a spell in a mental hospital or the church would've covered it up. They wouldn't have suffered the way Daniel did, or all the other boys did, or I did. Or the way Francesca did. I've spent my whole life blaming myself for my best friend's death. If I hadn't persuaded him to sneak out of school that day, then she wouldn't have caught us –"

"That was an excuse!" I cried angrily. "Gerbasi used it as an excuse. If it hadn't been that, it would've been something else. And you were little boys! It doesn't matter how bloody naughty you were, there was never any reason for him to do what he did to you. Other than the fact that he was a sick perverted bastard."

Will put his head in his hands. His voice was muffled and thick with tears.

"It doesn't matter now anyway, does it? They're all dead. All except one."

Even in my half-pissed emotional state, I managed to pull myself together.

"You mean Agostini?" I said. "But he's missing, isn't he? That's ruined your plans. "

"I never planned anything. Francesca did." He looked at me, sadly. "She even planned getting you here. I just helped."

I stared at him for a moment in shock. My whole world was falling to pieces.

"Tell me."

"Ok, but I need another drink first." He stood up and grabbed another bottle of wine, but I covered my glass.

"I won't," I said. "I'm finding this hard enough to take in as it is."

He downed another glass shakily, then began to talk.

Francesca had cried and cried until Will thought she couldn't possibly have any more tears in her. Finally freed of the burden of hating her, they'd hugged for a long time. It felt strange to feel something almost like love for this woman who'd helped make his childhood – and much of his adult life – a living hell, but there was also a feeling of peace and acceptance.

It lasted all of about five minutes after she began to tell him where Gerbasi was now, and what he was up to.

Will pleaded with her to take what she knew to the police, but she refused; she didn't have enough evidence to face someone as rich and powerful as Pio Agostini, who would have an army of lawyers ready to take her down before she'd even left the police station. Besides, she didn't want the poor boys who'd been affected to have to face a barrage of questions from adults. Will could understand why she felt like that, but he also knew that without their testimonies, the men would escape prosecution.

Even so, Will had balked at the idea of Francesca's more brutal, more final solution. He'd killed people during his time in the Army and it wasn't an experience he'd relished, despite it being the only option he'd had at the time.

Francesca realised she was losing her only ally. They talked about other things; about their recent lives and loves. And they talked about books. Will was a voracious reader. Long nights in Afghanistan, lying in bed in the relative safety of the Army compound listening to distant gunfire and the odd explosion, the inevitable sense of being a long way from home, both had been lessened by losing himself in a good book. Francesca spoke of her late husband and his work, and showed Will her own tome of ghost stories – gratified to hear that he'd actually picked up an English translation of it in his first week there.

The topic turned to favourite authors. And I was theirs. Both bemoaned the fact that I hadn't written anything in so long and was suffering from writer's block (I'd been quite vocal about it on social media, wailing about the fact that I was bored of London and needed inspiration. I made a note to cancel my Facebook account).

When Will told her that my first book, The Boy On The Beach, had saved his life, she knew how to hook him.

"So Francesca sent you her book – we thought from your previous work and from social media that you'd probably like it – and of course she dropped in the hint about you coming to stay in her apartment –"

A light bulb went on in my head.

"So that's how it came to my house, not my agent's office," I said. "Susie said it was weird. But you work for Interpol, so of course you could look up my address..."

Will had the decency to look shame faced. "Yes. But of course we didn't know for certain you'd come –"

My heart broke a little bit more as something else occurred to me. "When we met – it wasn't Fate, was it? It wasn't a happy accident. I thought to myself the other day how lucky we were to meet and fall in love –" I swallowed back my tears. It was all lies.

"The café – that *was* an accident. Francesca had booked you the gondola ride and printed out the wrong email thing and I was supposed to just be passing and swoop in to help, but I was early." Will took another gulp of wine. I wondered how much longer it would be before he was completely legless. *He'd better finish his fucking story first!* I thought, angrily.

"When I looked over and saw you that morning, I nearly passed out." Will smiled as he remembered. "I'd been working myself up to that scene at the gondola, but there you were, ordering coffee and smiling at me! And then, when you invited me to go on the gondola with you – I just wanted to sit there all day talking to you. I almost called the whole thing off. But I didn't want to let Francesca down, after all her planning. I thought, if you didn't go to Poveglia, I'd tell her it was off. But then you went, and..."

I blinked my tears away, annoyed at myself for still loving him, wanting all this to be a terrible misunderstanding, and still wanting to just sail away into the sunset with him.

"So I know how you got me here, but I don't understand why?"

"Francesca said that you'd saved me in the past, with your book, and that we had the chance to save you with hers. And get rid of a group of people who didn't deserve to live at the same time."

I scoffed incredulously. "Oh right, so you did it for me? It's my fault you strung someone up and almost decapitated them, is it? My fault you slit someone's throat and then shoved a carnival mask up their arse?"

Will looked hurt. "Bella, please, try and understand –"

"Don't come the hurt feelings with me, sonny Jim! You stuck someone's face in a deep fat fryer!"

"Francesca said –"

"Francesca's not fucking here to face the music, is she?" I was suddenly so furious that if she hadn't already been dead, I'd have killed her. "She's done it again. She manipulated you into doing her dirty work and then fucked off to leave you to take the blame on your own!"

"She hasn't 'fucked off', as you so delicately put it!" Will shouted back. "She killed herself! And she wasn't leaving me to face the music. That wasn't the plan."

"No? So what was the plan? They may have been bad people, the world may even be a better place without them in it, but I don't think the Mayor is going to give you the fucking key to the city, is he?"

Will stood up slowly and walked over to the bookcase, reaching up to the top shelf and taking down a copy of Francesca's book. He flicked through it until he reached the story he was looking for, and handed it to me.

The Tale of the Avenging Angels

There once in Heaven lived two angels. These angels had been with God from the beginning, formed from the ether and serving at His right hand. They would watch the Earth from their place in the firmament and report Mankind's achievements and failings to their Lord.

At first, they enjoyed their important work; but as time went on, and Mankind began to forget the Commandments and grow lazy, greedy and salacious, the angels began to despair. They despaired because they could see how unhappy this made God.

They despaired when they saw rich men take the bread from the mouths of the poor; despaired when they saw the strong punish the weak, rather than defend them; and despaired when they saw men turn their back on love for the sake of carnal pleasures. But their deepest despair was reserved for the suffering of little children.

One day the angels went to the Lord and asked him why it was that He never saw fit to punish the wrongdoers; to which he replied that, having given Man free will, it was down to Man to decide who to punish and who to reward.

They didn't like that answer.

Angels however have the power, should they so chose, to visit Earth and even become mortal. One day, unable to witness the suffering any longer, the angels took on mortal forms and joined Mankind on the Earth.

But although they were now mortals, they kept their angelic sense of justice; their new free will tempered by the knowledge that their Father waited for them in Heaven.

The angels went straight away to the houses of the biggest sinners and bestowed punishment on them, making examples of them in their suffering so that the rest of Mankind would take heed.

When God saw what they had done, His heart was filled with sorrow; he knew that they had brought sin upon themselves with their acts of unmerciful punishment, but he also knew why they had acted in this way. He visited the angels on Earth and told them that they must seek redemption in order to re-enter Heaven; by punishing the biggest sinners who now roamed the Earth. The angels trembled, but realised what they had to do; and turning their swords upon themselves, gained redemption.

I read that last line to myself three times.

"You and Francesca – you're the angels?"

197

Will nodded. "We were supposed to finish punishing the wrongdoers and then turn our swords upon ourselves –"

"But she checked out early," I finished. "She set you on this insane path and then couldn't see it through to the end!"

"It wasn't like that!" insisted Will. "She was with me when I killed the others –"

"You said you didn't kill them!" I said. He hung his head.

"I had to," he protested weakly. "Those horrible things – the fryer and the mask and everything – Francesca wanted to do those things while they were still alive. She wanted to watch them suffer. But I couldn't do it."

"Oh, you're sooo sensitive..."

"Fuck off, Bella. I've killed before, I take no pleasure in it. Not even in the deaths of those bastards. It was like putting down a rabid dog – I had to kill them but if I enjoyed it, that would make me as bad as them. Inhumane." He sat down abruptly, I think before he fell down. "She got Gerbasi to take her over to Poveglia – she told him it would be a good location for one of their horrible meetings..."

I didn't ask what went on at these 'meetings'.

"I hid in the bushes. Francesca's plan was to stun him, then string him up in the bell tower with the chain and let him swing, but I'd already decided I would step in and finish him first. She banged him over the head with a rock but the bastard wouldn't go down. He was so old and frail but he just stood there for ages while she hit him. He didn't even fight back. She kept on hitting him and hitting him until she was covered in his blood and he was dead. I had to prise the rock out of her fingers to stop her. And then the two of us hoisted his body up into the bell tower. You were supposed to look up and see him hanging there, but the chain was old and rusty and gravity took over."

I didn't want to picture it in my mind but I could, all too clearly.

"What about Carlevaro?" I asked.

"Roberto Carlevaro didn't just like young boys, he liked grown up ones too." Will was very matter-of-fact. "There aren't a lot of gay bars in Venice but there are places, if you know where to look. I picked him up and persuaded him that a quick one in his mask workshop would be the perfect end to a wonderful evening."

His hand trembled as he began to pour another glass of wine, but then he stopped and put the bottle down.

"We went back to his shop, and I pushed him against the wall. He liked that – said he enjoyed it rough. So I pulled his hair and slit his throat, just as Francesca came in. She was furious that I'd started without her..."

"*She* was furious? I don't suppose Carlevaro was over the moon about it, do you?"

He glared at me. "And then the priest. I hated that priest. I went to Mass at his church after Francesca told me about him. The way he watched his altar boys made me want to pummel the life out of him right there and then. But I still couldn't do what she wanted me to do -- no one should die that way, not even him. . When I realised that she'd turned on the fryer and was waiting for it to heat up, I bashed his head in with a rolling pin."

His story finished, he looked at me. "So what happens now?" he asked.

"Believe it or not, Will, I'm having a little bit of trouble processing this," I said sarcastically. "This morning I felt invincible. I'd almost finished my new book and it's really good, if I say so myself. But more than that, I was in love with what I thought was this wonderful man –"sarcasm could only carry me so far and I choked back a sob.

Will reached out to take my hand. "I'm still the same man you fell in love with," he said softly.

I yanked my hand away. "Hardly."

"Come on, you know me! I like – I like boats, and, and kittens, and cheese –"

"Just not all on the same cracker," I said sourly.

He laughed humourlessly. "Still making jokes."

"Yeah. Somebody once told me it was a coping mechanism."

We sat in silence for a moment. Calm. Quiet. Unlike the utter bloody turmoil in my head, stomach and heart. I felt sick. I wanted to scream and tear at my hair and claw at Will's face – and I wanted to go to bed with him and make love and never get up again. All at the same time.

I picked up the book again. "You said there was supposed to be another murder," I said, flicking through the pages to the story that came after the Faceless Priest. "This one?"

I held out the book to him and he took it, reluctantly.

"The False Witness," he said. "Yes."

"And that's Agostini? Why is he a false witness?" I asked.

"Because he's rich and well loved and when he lies, people believe him," said Will. "He lies about his charity – it's not for the benefit of the boys who go there, it's for his perverted friends. I did a background check on him. When Carlevaro got arrested for lewd behaviour with a minor, Agostini gave him an alibi. When Gerbasi volunteered to work at the charity, Agostini told the trustees that he knew him well and they didn't need to do a background check on him. If he hadn't done that, neither of them would've been allowed anywhere near those boys."

"And I'm assuming he shares the same sexual preferences as his nasty friends?"

"Yes," Will said. "One boy did come forward about ten years ago and reported him, but Agostini offered him a lot of money to shut up. The family was really struggling, so they took it. I can't blame them. No one would've believed them and it gave their son a good start in life. It meant he could keep the family boatyard going."

"Gino?" I asked. Will nodded. It made sense. Of course Will had involved Gino; he'd had to make sure my visit to Poveglia coincided with Gerbasi's murder.

We sat quietly for a moment.

"When was it supposed to happen?" I asked.

"Tonight. You've read the story. I was supposed to meet him at midnight outside Pittaluga's church –"

"And then what?"

"You've read the story."

"And then what?"

"You know –"

"You tell me. I want to hear you say it."

"I was supposed to cut his tongue out!" Will spat. "Ok? Francesca would've done worse – do you know what a Mafia neck tie is?" I shook my head. "It's when they slit someone's throat and pull their tongue down through it. I've seen it on Mafia victims in Sicily. They're still alive when it's being done."

"And that's what she wanted to do? Nice friends you have."

Will shook his head again. "You are so quick to judge –"

I laughed bitterly. "Hard not to judge a person who deep fries someone's face."

His anger subsided. His whole body subsided. "She was ill," he said. "I'm not making excuses for her – or maybe I am, I don't know. She was crazy, tortured, more than I am, and I'm pretty fucked up... She wanted payback for the horrible life she'd had. She never got over losing her son, even after she found him again. She missed out on his whole childhood. I know she wasn't the only victim, and I know she manipulated me into helping her – what can I say? -- I'm stupid and weak. But she did suffer. I went to see her, the night she killed herself –"

"The quiet man," I said. "I heard her shouting and shrieking at someone, but all I could hear was a low murmur in reply. That was you, wasn't it?"

He nodded. "It was a risk going there, and I didn't want you to hear me, but when she rang me she sounded so scared and desperate. She was crazy. She said that Gerbasi had come back to torment her –"

I thought of that horrible, gravelly voice I'd heard and shivered.

"He did," I said. Will stared at me, amazed. "He did. I heard him. And saw him, today, when I found her body."

Will shook his head slowly. "No...no, there's no such thing as ghosts..."

"What time did you leave Francesca that night?" I asked him.

"I don't know – about 3am? 3.15?"

"At 3.20 I heard a loud bang, which I now know was her kicking the chair away as she hung herself. And at 3.20 every night since, I've heard it again. Or dreamt of her."

Will shivered.

202

I took the book from his hands again and held it up.

"This book was Francesca's plan," I said. "So far, everyone's had a story – the killers and the victims, plus one intended victim. Anyone missing?"

He looked at me, not understanding.

"What about me? Do I have a story?"

CHAPTER TWENTY-FOUR

Will found the page and began to read.

The Sculptor and The Robbers

In the city long ago there lived a famous sculptor. His work was praised all over the country and fetched high prices. He had a beautiful wife, a big house, and a reputation as a perfectionist.

But this was in the time of the plague, and his wife caught the terrible disease. Despite the danger to himself, the sculptor nursed her, selling all of his beautiful works of art, his fine clothes and eventually even his house to buy medicines from the traders who came from far off lands. But none of them worked. The sculptor's wife died, leaving him broken hearted and alone.

His home and workshop gone, the sculptor relied for a while

on the charity of his former wealthy patrons, sculpting statues for them in return for food and shelter. But without his muse – his loving wife – the sculptor's hands lost their magic, and his talent all but disappeared. Eventually even his most loyal supporters gave up on him, and he was left to wander the streets begging for scraps.

The sculptor took to sleeping in the doorway of a church on a busy square, where he could sit in the shadows and watch life going on around him undisturbed. He soon became such a familiar sight to the residents of the square that after a while they stopped noticing he was even there. And as he watched them going about their daily business, the sculptor would carve their figures into the soft stonework around the church door, his talent still there under the layers of sadness that had engulfed him.

One night, a band of robbers came to the church. They had heard that the local noble families had joined together to buy a magnificent altar piece of solid gold, studded all over with fine gem stones. They broke into the church through a window at the rear, and were just making their way out when the priest arrived and caught them.

The priest called to God to help him stop the thieves, but the cowardly robbers, fearing that his loud cries would rouse the neighbourhood, beat him and left him bleeding to death in the doorway of the church while they made their escape.

But they reckoned without the sculptor, who had witnessed the whole thing. The poor man had spent so long sitting in the shadows, watching in silence, that he had forgotten how to speak; but when the local people came to the church in the morning and found the priest's body, they also found the entire story carved into the stone door surround. The murderous robbers were swiftly caught, and harshly dealt with, and news of the sculptor's hand in the arrest soon circulated.

The city elders awarded him his own workshop and before long he was back at work. Only now his sculpture was even more life-like than it had been before.

I listened as Will read out the story.

"I could see that ending coming a mile off," I joked, helplessly. "But I liked the bit where everyone deserted him and thought he was a loser. I can relate to that."

"What are you going to do now?" asked Will, watching me anxiously.

"Well, I'm not going to take up fucking sculpture," I said. I stood up. "I need some air."

I headed towards the door but Will leapt up and stood in front of me. I looked up at his eyes, nervous of him for the first time.

"Get out of my way please, Will," I said cautiously.

"Are you going to the police?" he asked. I shook my head.

"No. I don't know *what* I'm doing," I said. I felt completely helpless. "I just need some air. Please let me out, Will." I could feel hysteria starting to rise in me and cursed the fact that I am such a wimp and hypocrite, to boot.

"Whatever you decide to do, I'll understand." Will suddenly looked hopeless. Spent. No fight left in him. Like he just wanted it to be over. "I'll always love you, even if you hate me."

"I don't hate you!" I burst out. I had to get away from him before I totally lost it. I pushed him out of the way and ran out of the house, through the courtyard, out of the gate. I could hear him behind me.

I ran down the narrow, twisting passageway, then turned into another, and another... It was dark now – we'd been talking far longer than I'd realised – and I'd only been here once before, so it wasn't long before I was horribly lost. I ran along another street, turned a corner, and stopped short, a deep black canal in front of me.

I struggled for breath as I fought back the tsunami of tears that threatened to overwhelm me. And then gave up and drowned in it anyway.

In my head I saw the final scene of my book.

Chapter Dunno-the-number – last one – the end WIP (new working title: Dead in Venice)

Ella gazed out across the ocean, her mind lulled by the soothing rock of the waves. Behind her, Tom turned off the engine and they drifted silently for a while.

He reached out and took her hand, and she squeezed his, relishing the warmth and softness, marvelling at the thought that this man loved her so deeply that he was willing to entrust his future – his life – to her. She smiled at him, but inside her heart shattered into a million tiny pieces.

"I love you, Ella," he whispered, drawing her close. She could feel her resolve weakening, her love for him making this the hardest decision she'd ever have to make; yet in another way, it was also the easiest, because she couldn't imagine a future without him in it.

"I love you too," she said, kissing him tenderly. "But you can't get away with what you've done. Murder can never go unpunished."

He looked at her, tears in his eyes. And suddenly she knew; he was aware of exactly what her plan was.

"I know," he said. "It's all right, Ella. This is the only way."

They wrapped each other into the tightest, warmest embrace, then kissed again, one last time. Ella took a deep breath and closed her eyes, as together they tumbled off the boat into the icy cold depths of the sea, never to be parted.

I took a deep shaky breath and stared into the canal, the water blurred by my tears. I wiped them away, then jumped as in the reflection I saw Will looking back at me.

My heart leapt as for a second I thought that he'd jumped in and was looking up out of the water, but then I turned and he was there behind me.

"Don't – don't –" I stammered, then he took me into his arms, burying his face in my hair, his words coming out in a rush.

"I thought you were going to throw yourself in!" he cried. "All because of me – I'm the one who should –"

"Stop it!" I said, taking his face in my hands and staring into his eyes. "No more death. NO. MORE. Not this bloody False Witness, or you. And definitely not me. This is where it ends."

"Francesca planned it –"

"Fuck Francesca," I said firmly. "This isn't her story any more, it's ours."

We kissed passionately, then stood for a while in the moonlight, hugging each other fiercely.

"So what *do* we do now?" Will asked, finally.

"We rewrite the ending," I said. "Come back to my apartment, I need my laptop."

We walked back to Francesca's apartment, hand in hand, drunk not only on wine but on fear and relief and love and the sense that we would find a way out of this.

Police tape criss-crossed the door to the upstairs apartment. We looked at it, then each other. I shrugged. "She's gone," I said. We went inside.

Will made a pot of strong coffee as I flipped open the laptop and started to write.

I know it sounds like a weird thing to do – the love of my life has just been revealed as a serial killer but I still love him and need to find a way to help him, so I decide to finish my book... But actually I think better when I write. Not clearer, as such, just – better. It was going to take a creative solution and a half for him to get away with this. I ignored the tiny voice in my head that kept insisting that he *shouldn't* get away with it. *Sod off, tiny voice* I thought. *He's mine, I love him and he's suffered enough. We both have.*

It was very late by now, but the words were coming thick and fast. My fingertips flew across the keyboard, having a hard time keeping up with the flow of ideas bursting from my brain (writing doesn't often happen like that – more often it's like wringing out a very very dry sponge, trying to coax something out by sheer force and bloody-mindedness – but when it does, it's akin to the biggest and best orgasm you've ever had. Actually, it was like the biggest and best orgasm I'd ever had previous to meeting Will. Sigh).

And then it was done. I was spent. No more words. I slumped over the laptop.

"Are you ok?" asked Will, waking abruptly from his nap on the sofa.

"More than ok," I said. "I just finished another best seller."

"Can I read it?" Will leapt up eagerly.

I laughed. "Ok, but it's probably full of typos and spelling mistakes and there's quite possibly a massive plot hole around chapter eighteen..."

He elbowed me gently out of the way and sat in front of the laptop. I laughed and kissed him. "I'm going for a lie down," I said.

CHAPTER TWENTY-FIVE

I didn't expect to fall asleep. I was exhausted – it was past midnight by now and it had been a long and tiring day (understatement of the century), but my head was still whirling, coming to terms with what Will had done, and with the fact that I didn't care what he'd done, which was a bit of a revelation to me in itself. Who'd have thought I could forgive a serial killer? It helped that his victims were unmitigated bastards, but even so – it was a big ask.

But I loved him, more than I'd ever loved anyone else, and I wanted to look after him. I wanted to hug him tightly and tell him that everything was going to be ok, that I would take care of it and of him.

I didn't look at the clock as I fell asleep, but it must've been nearly 3.20am.

Gerbasi was waiting for me. He didn't even pretend to still have his head attached; he held it under one arm in a way that I felt was a terrible ghost cliché, but then how would I know? I'd only ever lost my head in a metaphorical way.

"Oh for – why are you still here?" I asked him, angrily. "I know who killed you, and why, and quite frankly I don't blame him. I'd have done the same thing myself."

"No you wouldn't," said Gerbasi's head. It was weird, talking to someone's disembodied head. I wasn't entirely sure where to look. "Oi! Eyes down here!"

"Sorry," I said. "This is a new experience for me."

"Believe it or not, it's not something I've done before either," Gerbasi's head noted sourly.

"Fair point. But still – can't you head (no pun intended) towards the light or something now?" I asked. "You shouldn't still be in limbo or whatever you call it."

Gerbasi's body held his head out in front of him and shook it impatiently.

"I don't know," the head said. "You still don't get it, do you? This isn't limbo, you half wit, this is a dream."

"No need to get sarky, doctor. You're 'ahead' of me on this one."

"I don't think that's very funny." The doctor's head turned around in a huff, followed a couple of seconds later by the rest of his body.

I felt a chill behind me and shivered as an icy breath whispered in my ear.

"Finire la mia storia!"

I whirled around to see Francesca standing behind me, her face purple, neck bruised, eyes bulging slightly. Hanging does a woman's appearance absolutely no favours.

"And you can cut that out!" I said angrily. "I am finishing the story, but it's not yours any more, it's mine. Mine and Will's."

She shook her head sadly.

"I had such high hopes for that young man," she said, "but he let me down."

"Let you down?" I was amazed. "He killed three men for you! He was going to kill himself as well!"

"Yes, but then you stopped him!" she hissed, her eyes suddenly blazing with anger. "He should be here, now, with me! But now I'll have to spend eternity alone with my brother!"

"I know," I said, calmly. "Families, huh? Who'd have them?"

She shrieked angrily and flew at my face, but I stood my ground.

"This is a dream," I said. "I am so out of here."

And I woke up.

Moonlight streamed in through the shutters at the bedroom window, reflecting the ripples on the canal. I watched them dance on the ceiling, mesmerised, still half asleep.

A shadow appeared, adrift on those ripples. It grew larger and larger until it filled my vision and features formed. Wild hair, bulging eyes, purple face; Francesca.

She shrieked in fury and flew at my face again, but this time I couldn't wake up; this time it wasn't a dream. Her hands hooked into claws, her talon fingernails ploughing down my face as she screamed at me, over and over again: *"Finire la mia storia! Finire la mia storia!"*

I struggled upright, shoving her as hard as I could, and reached for the nearest objects to hand on my bedside table, bringing them together in the shape of a cross.

"Fuck off Francesca! You're a terrible writer and I'm finishing the story the way I want it to end!" I yelled. "I'm giving us a happy ending!"

The Francesca harpy screamed in pain and began to smoke around the edges, flames starting to catch at the floaty nightgown she wore. Just as the fire grew in intensity, she imploded, disappearing inwards with a POP! Leaving nothing behind her but a slight smoky haze in the air.

I looked down at the cross I held in my trembling hands and laughed, though shakily. I was holding the last two writers' awards I'd won.

"Bella! Bella, wake up!" I opened my eyes and looked up into Will's frightened face. I smiled at him and he breathed out, a deep sigh of relief.

"Thank god for that!" he said.

"What's the matter, sweetheart?" I asked, looking around the room, just to make sure we were alone. There were no writers' awards on my bedside table – they were back in my study in London - and no hint of smoke, fire or brimstone lingered in the air.

"I came in to check on you, and you were writhing about and moaning," he said.

I raised an eyebrow. "You've seen me writhing about and moaning before," I said.

He laughed and leaned into kiss me, then lay down next to me.

I propped myself up on one elbow and looked at him.

"So? Did you read it? What do you think?"

He smiled and stroked the hair away from my face.

"It's perfect. It's not even really about the murders, is it? It's about you and me."

"It's a love story," I said. "With a couple of gruesome murders, admittedly, but..."

We smiled at each other for a moment, wondering which of us would broach the subject of the ending. Eventually I had to.

"So, did you like the ending?"

He nodded, his smile becoming sad. "It's just right."

I swallowed. Now was the time to apply it to our situation.

"So, now we have to work out our own ending –"

"Not that one," said Will, firmly.

"But we get to be together forever –"

"Not like that."

"But it's easy! We get a boat –"

"I've got a boat."

"No, we get a bigger boat and we just sail away. We disappear! I've got money – I've got a *lot* of money. We could do it –"

"Bella!" he reached out and put a finger to my lips. "I'm glad your book ended the way it did. For a while I thought they were going to make some kind of suicide pact and throw themselves into the canal, but I like the characters so much I didn't want them to die. I'm glad they got away."

"So why can't we –"

"Because in real life, I can't get away with murder."

"Even if the victims deserved it?"

"Even then. You nailed it, ages ago. No one has the right to appoint themselves judge, jury and executioner. And that's what I did."

"I also said that sometimes it's the only way to see Justice served."

"And you really believe that?" he asked.

I looked at him for a moment, wondering if I was really going to say what I thought I was going to say. But what did I have to lose?

"Yes. I have to believe it. Because it's the only way I can live with what I did."

"What are you talking about?" Will looked puzzled. "What did you do?"

I took a deep breath. I was finally going to tell another person the secret I'd been carrying around with me since I was seven years old, the secret known only to me and my sister. "I killed someone too."

When I was seven years old and my sister Megan was five, our parents split up. You already know that.

Our mum was a nurse, and she worked shifts at the local hospital. Sometimes she had to work overnight. Our dad lived nearby so whenever he could, he'd stay over and look after us, or we'd go and sleep at his tiny flat, cuddling up on the sofa bed in his living room and whispering to each other. It was fun. It felt like camping out.

But occasionally his job involved travel, which meant that sometimes there was no one to watch us. Luckily, Mum was friendly with the old couple who lived next door, the Harrisons. Mrs Harrison was sweet and grey haired and used to feed us pink and white coconut ice until our teeth would start to ache with all the sugar. Mr Harrison was funny and chatty, and he used to sing silly little songs to make us laugh.

He also used to touch us.

It started off with just me. He never raped me, exactly; if you want to get clinical about it, penile penetration never took place between me, the seven year old girl who loved her teddy bears, and him, the seventy-odd year old man who should've fucking known better. But he used to touch me over my dress, then under my dress and over my knickers, then under my knickers... And he used to make me touch him, too. I hated it. I hated him. But I liked Mrs Harrison and I couldn't believe that she'd be married to someone that horrible. I decided it must be my fault. I must be doing something to make him act like that, and if I told anyone they wouldn't believe me, or they'd realise that I was an awful person.

And then he started on Megan. My little sister. She would cry so hard afterwards, which made me realise that if I didn't do something to protect her, I really *was* an awful person. When Mum wasn't there (and she was so busy, and had so much on her plate that I didn't want to worry her), when it was just the two of us, Megan was my responsibility. But what could I do?

One night, Mr Harrison – even now, saying his name leaves a rancid taste in my mouth – was watching us while Mum was at work and Mrs Harrison was at the Bingo. He had angina, and he had medication that he kept with him at all times in case of an attack. After his usual fun and games with us he settled down in the armchair to watch 'Family Fortunes' while Megan and I cried ourselves to sleep.

Except this time, I didn't go to sleep. I crept downstairs and took the medication from the pocket of his jacket, which was hanging over the stair banister, and took it upstairs.

An hour or so later, I heard him gasping for breath. I crept out of my bed, clutching the stolen medication, and tiptoed to the top of the stairs. The old bastard was frantically searching through his jacket pockets for his pills. I gripped the packet tighter, watching him clutch at his chest, scrabbling at it as if he was trying to pull his heart out to stop the pain with a look of horror and panic on his face. He looked up and spotted me watching him from the shadows, and called out to me.

"Bella, there's a good girl! Get the phone! Call an ambulance!"

I just stood there, watching him.

"Bella?" I turned round and there was Megan, eyes red rimmed with sleepy tears. I pulled her to me, hugging her tight so she wouldn't have to see Mr Harrison dying at the bottom of the stairs.

"Come on Meggy, back to bed!" I said. She craned her neck to see what was going on but I led her back to the bedroom and shut the door.

Mum didn't take us to the funeral. We were upset enough at the death of the kindly old neighbour, she said. But we did go and see Mrs Harrison afterwards. Their grown up daughter, who had left home at 18 and rarely came back for a visit, was there. She looked right into my eyes and, even though I was only seven, I realised that she knew what he'd done to us, because he'd done it to her too. She hugged me tight and said everything would be ok now.

I finished speaking and looked at Will, who sat there with his mouth open so wide he was in danger of dislocating his jaw.

"Say something, please," I begged. "You're the only person I've ever told."

He laughed gently. "It explains a lot. Like why you didn't run for the hills when you found out what I'd done. You're as screwed up as I am."

"I'm not screwed up. I just think that sometimes, good people can do bad things, but for a good reason." I was aware that that sounded like a trite excuse, but I meant it.

Will took my hands in his and looked serious. "Bella, you were a frightened little girl. You didn't kill him. You weren't to know he'd have a heart attack. What I've done is rather different."

"No it isn't!" I cried. "Well, yeah it is, but –"

He smiled at me and tenderly stroked my face.

"Thank you for telling me your story, Bella. I think you were very brave. But it doesn't change anything. It's my turn to be brave now."

I blinked back hot tears. I'd cried more in the last day than I had in the last two years. I was amazed I still had any moisture left in me and hadn't turned into a desiccated husk.

"So what are you going to do?" I asked, fearing the answer.

"Oh don't worry, I'm not going to turn my angelic sword on myself," he laughed softly. "I'm going to hand myself in to Manera. He's a good man, a friend, and if I talk to him and explain the situation, he'll deal with me fairly."

"You'll get life in prison," I said, beginning to cry. He shrugged.

"Maybe. Maybe not as long as that. There were extenuating circumstances, weren't there? Who knows? But it's not down to me or you to make that judgement."

I stared into his eyes. After all the tears and distress of the last 24 hours, he was calm. Calmer than I was, anyway. He'd accepted responsibility for his horrific part in the murders and was resigned to his fate, to his punishment. I was pretty sure that if I pleaded and begged and cried and seduced him, then I could manipulate him into changing his mind and running away with me. But I wasn't going to do that, no matter how much it broke my heart, because I loved him.

"Ok," I said, and we were both crying pretty freely by now. "But do you have to go right now? I want to stay here and pretend for a little while that everything is going to be ok."

We held each other tightly, then kissed and made gentle, tender love to each other. And then, hearts aching, we made our way to the police station.

CHAPTER TWENTY-SIX

We took a water taxi to the Piazzale Roma and stepped onto the Ponte della Liberta, the road bridge that connects the island to the mainland. We reached the police station, a large stone walled enclave with an unimposing white porch entrance, too quickly.

I tugged at Will's hand, stopping him.

"You sure about this?" I asked. *Please change your mind* I thought, knowing that he wouldn't.

He nodded, then he took a deep breath and we walked inside.

Inside it was chaos. In the foyer, Manera stood in front of a group of reporters, TV cameras rolling, microphones in his face, cameras flashing. He was too far away for us to hear his words properly, and in any case they were in Italian so I'd have been none the wiser anyway.

Will showed his Interpol ID to the officer on the door and asked him what was going on.

"*Conferenza stampa,*" the officer replied, looking over at the crowd and shrugging; no need to ask what he thought of the journalists scrabbling around for a story.

The officer showed us through the crowd towards a back room. As we worked our way through the throng, Manera spotted us and nodded. It was clear that the press conference was ending. "Ah, Agent Carmichael!" Manera called out, in a much friendlier tone than I'd previously heard from him. "And Signora Tyson."

"You know who I am?" I asked, surprised. He laughed.

"Signora, I've always known who you are. Please, come this way." He led us through a busy incident room, talking to passing officers and looking back at us.

"This is very fortunate," he said. "I was about to call you, Agent Carmichael."

"Oh yes?" Will and I exchanged curious looks.

"As you see I have just been talking to the press. We have made an arrest in connection with the Gerbasi case."

Will ground to a halt in shock. "You've what?"

Manera smiled. "You didn't think we were investigating the matter very thoroughly? You didn't think we'd find the murderer?"

"No, it's not that –" stammered Will.

Manera looked around, his smile disappearing for a moment.

"Perhaps we should talk in my office."

He opened a door and stood back to let us in. The room was small, with a cluttered desk, but it had a view of the Grand Canal to make up for it. I glanced at his desk as he gestured for us to take a seat, spotting a folder perched on top of a teetering pile; it was marked 'Francesca Vialli'. Manera saw me and quickly took the folder and buried it in the pile.

"I wanted to see you, Inspector – Sergio –" Manera looked alarmed as Will nervously spoke and stopped him.

"Yes, and as I said, it is fortunate that you did as we have solved the murders." Manera smiled widely and falsely. "We have the perpetrator in the cells at this moment. He gave us a full confession –"

"He did?" Will was amazed. I looked at Inspector Manera and had a light bulb moment. At least, I hoped it was a light bulb moment and not just a stupid idea -- otherwise I was going to look really, well, stupid.

"Who's the culprit?" I asked.

"His name is Pio Agostini –"

Will's jaw, already open, dropped even further in amazement.

"The restaurateur, yes? You know him?" Manera asked.

"But how –" The wind had truly been taken out of Will's sails.

"It is a terrible story, a scandal. You will read about it in the papers, I think," said Manera. "He disappeared after the murder in his restaurant, which is definitely a sign of guilt –"

"Or just fear that he was going to be the next victim," Will pointed out. I shook my head at him: *shut up!*

Manera said, "But you see he was an acquaintance of all three victims and it seems that there are certain irregularities in the running of his children's charity."

"I see," I said. I was certain I was right now. "By the way, I am so sorry about your mother."

Will looked at me in astonishment, then at Manera, who just smiled thinly.

"Yes," he said. "It was a tragedy as we had only just got to know each other. I was adopted, as you no doubt are aware."

Will shook his head, to clear it. "Are you telling me you're Francesca's son?"

I did a mini fist-pump. "Yes, he is!" I looked at Manera and said, 'I knew you recognised Gerbasi when Will gave you his wallet that day."

"Congratulations on your brilliant detective work," said Manera sardonically. "But do remember that I have just lost my mother."

We all sat and stared at each other for a moment, at a loss how to proceed.

Finally Will said, "Look, I have to know something. Other than this confession, is there any actual evidence to tie Agostini to the murders? Without DNA evidence -"

"Will!" I hissed at him. "What the hell are you doing? This –"

"This lets the real murderer off the hook," Manera smiled wryly. "Is that what you were about to say?"

"Er –"

He laughed. "Can I let you into a secret, signora? My mother, as you may or may not know, told me all about that pig Gerbasi and his disgusting friends. I wanted to prosecute them, but couldn't see how to do it – "

He paused and I said quickly, "How to do it without ruining the career you'd worked so hard to build? Accusing a man of Agostini's power and influence, no doubt lawyered up to the teeth – that could come back to bite you on the backside, yes?" I asked.

Manera smiled grimly. "Yes, there was a little of that. But mostly how to do it without dragging my mother's name and reputation through the mud. I was horrified at her part in my uncle's past crimes, but I could see how much she had suffered. And I knew that there were innocent victims out there who did not deserve to be subjected to a trial, especially when a conviction was far from guaranteed."

He got up and stared out of the window. It seemed unreal to think that outside there people were going about their business -- shopping, arguing, falling in and out of love, getting their hair done, while in here ...

"I told my mother that I would deal with them, but she didn't believe me. She thought I was too much by the book to do anything. In the mean time I had to distance myself from her."

"Why?" I asked.

"I did not want there to be any obvious connection between myself and the victims."

"But at that point," said Will, slowly, "You didn't know that they would be victims. Unless -"

Manera smiled grimly at him. "Agent Carmichael, you know as well as I do how easy it is to get lost in the streets of Venice at night. You can imagine how easy it would be for someone to have too much to drink and end up at the bottom of a canal."

We both stared at him in amazement. He laughed. "You look shocked. How long have you been in Italy, Agent Carmichael? How many Mafia cases have you investigated? And yet you still don't realise that in our culture family is more important than anything else. Someone hurts your family, you have the right to make them pay for it. And when a member of your family transgresses in such a way as my uncle did, it is your duty to make them pay."

"So – you were going to –" I couldn't believe it but it was clear that he was serious.

"My uncle's filthy cabal would have ended up at the bottom of the canal, one by one." Manera shook his head in mock

225

consternation. "So many tragic accidents! And my uncle would have been left, the only one knowing the real reason why those men had died, and knowing that his turn would be coming next."

He threw up his arms in exasperation. "And then of course the circus came to town! Before I could quietly go about my family business, a madman –"

"Encouraged by an elderly madwoman," I pointed out, gently but firmly.

He nodded. "Yes, I realise that – they blunder in, all guns blazing, and turn it into a spectacle! And then a famous author comes along to chronicle the whole thing! *Mamma mia!*"

He shook his head. "It would have made the murders very difficult to write off as accidents, with you poking around."

We looked at each other for a moment, then I giggled nervously.

"Some accident!" I said.

"Exactly. But luckily the real culprit – Agostini - doubtless he felt the weight of his sins and decided he could no longer support these men. So he killed them and ran away before we could trace his relationship with them." Manera looked at Will. "A good thing that he did, because we could not get any DNA evidence from any of the crime scenes. We had no leads, no clues as to the murderer or murderers."

Will opened his mouth to speak. I so wanted him to just shut up.

"I have to confess –"

"- that you didn't have any leads either," said Manera quickly, "I understand."

"But –"

"Will darling," I said sweetly. "Shut the fuck up now and listen to the Inspector."

Manera smiled at me. "Exactly so. The murderer is in custody, the case is closed."

"But lack of evidence –" Will wouldn't shut up, no matter how hard I glared at him.

"Lack of evidence will not be a problem," said Manera. "It will not go to court. Agostini hanged himself in his cell, another admission of his guilt."

"Oh my god, when did that happen?" I asked, surprised. The Inspector looked at his watch.

"In about half an hour."

Will and I stared at him in shock. He became business-like again, the Inspector we were used to. He picked up Francesca's file and shuffled through it. "And now if you would excuse me, I am very busy. I have my mother's funeral to organise. Do have a good trip back to England."

"We're not going back to England," said Will, bewildered.

"Oh yes we bloody are," I said. "Good day to you, Inspector."

CHAPTER TWENTY-SEVEN

I t started at the door, then snaked its way along the street and
round the corner. It got in the way of mothers with
pushchairs, elderly ladies pulling shopping trolley bags behind
them, and a young hipster guy on his phone who wasn't looking
where he was going. It smelt of take away coffee and perfume, of
brand new books and bored children and e-cigarettes, and moved
at a snail's pace, shuffling backwards and forwards to let people in
and out of the shops that lined its path and on and off the buses
that plied their trade up and down the Charing Cross Road.

When you leave it such a long time between books there's
always a worry that people will forget about you, so it was
gratifying to see the queue of people waiting outside the bookshop
and beyond. My fans are very loyal. Some more than others.

Susie and Guy had welcomed me back from Venice with
open arms and excited smiles, desperate to read this new book
that I was (modestly) raving about. I'm not arrogant – I'm like
most writers; sometimes I think I'm good, sometimes I *know* I'm

good, and other times I am literally the worst writer in the world ever and should be physically restrained from ever using a laptop or computer or typewriter or even a fucking pen.

But most of the time I know I'm good.

It hadn't hurt either that my new book, Dead in Venice, was inspired by a series of true events. Although I was keeping exactly how accurate a portrayal of those events it was, firmly under my hat.

I sat at the desk, surrounded by cardboard cut- outs of Venetian landmarks including a bell tower, although it looked more like San Marco's than Poveglia's. Could this day get any more surreal?

The doors opened and the shop was flooded with eager book lovers. I took a deep breath, grabbed my pen and steeled myself.

"Thank you so much for coming ... yes, I loved Venice ... thank you ... so kind ... who's it to?" I made small talk, smiled, had selfies taken with fans, signed a lot of books, smiled some more .... It seemed so far removed from where I'd been only twelve months previously – contemplating disappearing into the wide blue yonder with a man I'd known less than a month.

A woman in big round glasses and a ridiculously fluffy jumper stood in front of the desk, holding out a copy of the book. "I've already read it!" she gushed. "It's fantastic! So much more romantic than your DCI Fletcher books."

"Yes," I smiled. "Between you and me, DCI Fletcher was starting to get on my nerves. Get it on with Viktor, already!"

She giggled. "Oh my god yes! But Tom is a much dreamier hero than Viktor. He's so sweet!"

"Yes," I sighed. "I'm so in love with Tom..."

I wrote a dedication in her book but she lingered a while longer.

"Is there going to be a sequel?" she asked. "Ella and Tom are such a lovely couple, I'd love to see more of them."

"I'm sure there will be –"

"Ooh, and set it somewhere exotic again!" she trilled. "It has such an exciting, romantic setting; it made me want to pack a suitcase and go to Venice myself!"

I laughed. "I haven't really thought about that yet –"

I felt a gentle hand on my shoulder and looked up into the eyes of my sweet, loving but still slightly damaged new husband, who was smiling down at me and my enthusiastic fan.

"How about New York?" suggested Will. "There are 200 unsolved murders in New York City every year. Who's going to notice a couple more?"

THANKS AND ACKNOWLEDGEMENTS

First of all I need to thank my husband and daughter, for putting up with me and letting me persuade them to take the annual family holiday in Venice – twice. Our first trip inspired this book, but I needed to go back after I'd written it to doublecheck a few locations and to eat more gelato. Research truly is hell.

I also owe a huge debt of thanks to the friends I've made through the online writing community. Extra special thanks go to the two greatest cheerleaders a woman could ever hope for, Carmen Radtke and Jade Bokhari. You ladies are the wind beneath my wings and you have kept me as sane as it's possible for a writer to be. I am very lucky to have you! There are many other great writers who have helped me with reading and feedback. You know who you are, and I owe you.

I want to thank my wonderful agent Lina Langlee at Kate Nash Literary Agency, and Audible, who published 'Dead in Venice' as one of their Crime Grant Finalists in 2018. Your faith in me has kept me going.

And last but not least, I want to thank the city and people of Venice. You are my spiritual home, and I'll be back.

Manufactured by Amazon.ca
Bolton, ON

24182411R00129